To Arnda

Let a Smile be your umbrella. Love yo,

Euple's Song

Euple Riney

Love Euple

Edited by
Regina Williams

AWOC.COM Publishing
Denton, Texas

Published by AWOC.COM Publishing, P.O. Box 2819, Denton,
TX 76202, USA. No part of this publication may be reproduced,
stored in a retrieval system, or transmitted in any form or by any
means, electronic, mechanical, recording or otherwise, without
the prior written permission of the author.

Manufactured in the United States of America

ISBN: 978-0-937660-36-2

Table of Contents

Dedication

Memory Lane

I don't expect my book to be taken by storm by any stretch of the imagination, or get any important reviews from a well-known publisher such as the New York Times. My punctuation is terrible; sometime there are run-on sentences and clumsy attempts to phrase a sentence just right. My spelling isn't worth a hoot and I have to check the dictionary to be sure. These words haven't come from years of study—but years of experience as a country girl who never did great deeds of valor, nor traveled to faraway places.

Over eight decades have passed and I've spent years—at least seventy-six years—poring over hundreds of books on various subjects, learning many lessons by trial and error.

I never went to college or earned a PhD. If my feeble efforts has any effect on friends and loved ones, that is enough for me. I came from a little girl in the 1920's, to a teenager, a wife, mother, and grandmother, who was busy changing diapers, wiping snotty noses and drying childish tears. I've also feed and reared five children, and held grandchildren in my embrace. Many tears I've shed and have also loved and laughed and held treasures in my work worn hands I never dreamed of.

My daughter, Regina, gets a big part of any success I may have achieved. She's never given up on me, always pushing me a little farther on. I could never have done it without her expertise, or my family's love.

I tried to keep in mind that the Lord is the main character in this book. It is through him I've been able to sling words together in some fashion. I've attempted to paint a picture of life and hope to my readers. (A picture is worth a thousand words.)

Happiness has been the theme, "Down Memory Lane." On one of my many adventures, I had the privilege of listening to the Jackson Hill Band at the Wild Horse Saloon in Nashville, Tennessee. It was a great adventure and one I wouldn't have missed for the world. Kris, Josh, Hoovey and Ben—you guys were awesome. Thanks for the once in a lifetime experience!

Euple's Song

The Lord is my strength and my song; he also has become my salvation. Isa. 12:2

From early childhood, singing from the depth of a joyful heart became my strength and often my salvation. A little girl's dreams were magic as I fantasized singing before a huge multitude in a great cathedral, my name in lights. When I grew up however, that dream faded into my own little cathedral, surrounded by a very loving audience with shining eyes and a heart full of love. "Just as I Am," Mama was Kate Smith all over again who performed daily just for them. That kept the *Joy Bells Ringing*.

"There's no place like home," floated in and around our little domain known as the Riney Kingdom in our own little open air theater where my voice did actually reach a multitude of listeners. There were eighty acres of trees and numerous hills where my voice echoed in the backwoods of Arkansas in harmony with the songbirds. My vast audience clapped their limbs with glee and the hills resounded with music.

My name never appeared in lights, but the voices of my children when they said, "Sing to me, again. I love you, Mama," outshone Broadway a thousand times over. A whisper of love between two lovers was not a fanciful dream. *This Little Light of Mine* was enough to spur me on, putting my dreams to naught, realizing my childhood dreams were only a prelude to my destiny of being a good wife and a loving mother.

Catchy little tunes were a lullaby for five babies. *This Little Boy (or Girl) of Mine, Danny Boy, Mammy's Little Baby Loves Shortening Bread, Rock-a-Bye-Baby*, and many others. The rhythm of a straight-backed kitchen chair hitting the floor, rocking and singing, touched the roof of our little cabin and wove its magic as a tiny face was buried into the crook of mama's arm. *Sleep Baby Sleep* was the theme song for a sleepy, tired little boy or girl. Tenderly laying them in the cradle, they never heard the last strains of Mama's Song.

All the responsibilities of a young wife and mother often brought unknown fears in the darkness of night, robbing me of sleep. With the coming of daybreak, however, those old fears

6

disappeared and sunlight brought a message of hope to my wavering heart. "This is the day the Lord has made, rejoice and be glad in it." Looking down from my cabin in the sky, those words lodged in my soul, causing me to sing with a greater joyful hope—My God, *How Great Thou Art.*

Songs of Zion became my salvation at the time of grief and sorrow after my beloved husband passed away. Yet for days afterward, my song died within me and was lost in the avenue of escape. Sorrow pulled the chains of my heart and I heard the stinging words of *Don't You Hear the Bells Now Ringing?* Calling the prodigal home. With my children and grandchildren's love surrounding me they heard and understood my last farewell, *I'll Meet You in the Morning.* Hearing love's ole sweet song, after a long passage of time, I could sing once again—*You Are My Sunshine.*

I sang we are going down the valley one by one as other members of our family followed on the path that leads to the road *At the End of the Way. In the Sweet By and By*, everything will be all right. *He'll Understand and Say Well Done*, when the *Roll is Called Up Yonder.*

Each morning as the sun rose out of its huge cradle, fully dressed in all its brilliant colors, I meet the dawn with, in the morning of joy, in the morning of joy when we'll get together on the morning of joy. When the shadows of evening lengthened, the call to suppertime rolled over the landscape. *Sweet Hour of Prayer* was the familiar salvation where our roots ran deep in the soil of the farm. All the farm animals bedded down in comfort for the night as the melody of my song, *Can I Sleep in your Barn Tonight Mister,* bounded off the barn roof.

Sweeping Through the Gate, was my last conscious thought as the lights went out in our mansion on the hilltop. *His Love is My Song.*

I belted out *Stormy Weather*, on a rainy day for I knew in my heart, *Love Will Roll the Clouds Away. Sunlight, Sunlight*, all along the way, *Since the Savior Found Me*, and took away my sins. I have the sunlight of His love within. I crooned, Sweet *Beulah Land, Just Beyond the Sunset*, as *Amazing Grace* filled my soul. I clapped my hands and sang Glory.

In *The Little Church in the Wildwood*, I raised my voice with other believers as the songs of Zion burst forth and bubbled up in my thirsting heart that was never actually filled. Like an addict, I have never been satisfied, always looking for another song.

I'm Looking That Way, I'll Live There Someday, On the Beautiful Hills of God, He Whispers Sweet Peace to Me, When I Wake Up to Sleep No More, Just A Closer Walk With Thee, In the Sweet By and By, I'm Gonna Shout and Shine.

Reaching stardom at long last, I'll sing with the multitude that makes up the symphony of heaven's jubilee, where dreams do come true.

My first book *Reflections*

There is Music in Them Thar Hills

Music echoes over the hills of Arkansas the third week of April, like a hundred drum rolls, while the trumpet from heaven announces an April concert. Spring steps out on stage wearing her bright green gown (a Paris original would be envious) sporting dancing shoes on her feet.

She flings out her arms in a welcome salute and says, "Come and see. 'Tis spring, 'tis spring." Trees put on brand new coats as they dip and sway to the music of a frolicking new song, as they Jitterbug on a soft multi-colored carpet. A blue sky sprinkled with white fluffy clouds is parading across an endless canvas. The lazy old sun is rolling around in its orbit all day long warming up the land in its embrace.

Wildflowers that had lain under a blanket of snow stretched their pretty heads toward the warmth in blooming splendor. They seem to say, "See, I'm the prettiest of them all. The Great Director knew I would one day deck the halls of royalty or grace the tables of the poor.

The concert is never complete until the return of the birds that performs on cue. The mockingbird sets high on a branch in an oak tree, mocking and mimicking other species. A born showman, what he lacks in color, he makes up for in grace and song.

The cardinal wears a red cape, and is the king of the Opera House. Others bow in his presence as he presides from his royal seat. The bobwhite lounges at the edge of the amphitheater, yet he wants everyone to know his name is Bobwhite—Bobwhite—Bobwhite. His sleeping quarters is a soft feather bed on the ground floor.

The tiny little hummingbird is like a flighty child, never still, yet he steals a sip of nectar from a flower as he darts from view. He is a greedy little rascal, for he is always fighting his siblings away from the dinner table.

The blue jay wears his colorful blue outfit and sits around scolding everyone. If they don't jump to his orders, they are apt to get a cuff on the head or back. If that doesn't work—then he tries another trick he is very good at—dive bombing the offender. The bluebird goes quietly around his home turf, bothering no one. His neighbors welcome him from a-far. No one wants to disturb his hour of house cleaning in preparation of the serenade.

The barn swallow is always preening and fluffing her pretty garment. Like a bride getting ready for her big day, she is practically a member of the Riney family, as she builds her house outside near the patio, year after year. There is always something happening around the Riney house that keeps the bird family bustling in and out all day long.

Spring starts the shoes dancing and the enzymes to flow. Talented harpist fingers plucks the strings of the new season that tickles the ears of the angels holding court, giving out a round of applause.

The sound of a big brass horn rolls over these hills, as it announces the Grand Entry that wakes up the frog choir. The little peepers are jumping and hopping along their favorite watery bed alongside rivers, creeks and ponds. Croaking out a love ballad—ribbit—ribbit—ribbit, they blend in well with the bass voice of the old bull frog. Bar-rum—bar-rum, happy and contented while he laps up the bugs. So, Froggy went a'courting.

The woodpecker wearing his colorful head gear reminds one of a soldier at war, gliding in silently, he fires off a volley of machine-gun bullets, as he hones in on an unsuspecting foe with a rat-a-tat-tat. The adversary doesn't know what hit them. Then he dines on the delicacies he plunders. Ah, yes, birds are the biggest attraction of the season, a bird-watchers Eden, while the band plays on in harmony with the gentle breeze.

As night falls, when the grand finale is over and the curtain comes down on another great performance, and darkness closes its huge door, then the stalker's of the night begin to prowl, looking for the spoils left behind. Midnight haunts the land as the stars come out to play while the big yellow moon is cavorting gaily around its huge playground, silently watching the entire wild kingdom dining out for supper. Mystery and intrigue walks the forest floor as dozens of coyotes lift their voice in a mating call, answered by many eligible females. Bats doing their acrobatic feats, dip and twist, catching juicy bugs unaware, under a canopy of fireflies that produce their own city of a million lights. The sly old fox is concentrating on a big fat hen from the farmer's chicken house. His mouth begins to salivate.

Mr. Terrapin, who never gets in any hurry, slowly pushes his cumbersome mobile house around. If an intruder gets too close, he simply goes inside and locks the door. Yet he leaves his calling card by crushing my lady's pansies and violets.

The old reptile is slipping through the underbrush intent on murder and mayhem, catching Mr. Rabbit off guard, then dines on fast food. Sluggish and full, he crawls under a boulder or bush, ready to strike again. The law of the forest—only the swiftest and toughest survive.

Deer and their offspring dine on green pastures as darkness hides them from a hunter's eye intent on doing harm to their tribe. At the least noise, they spring along on racing feet under the cover of darkness.

On the other hand, romance rides on the crust of spring like so many young brides flaunting her wedding gown for all to see. Music of the wind is provided for the wedding ceremony as it whispers, "I do."

Ah, yes, the Great Director is conducting the ebb and flow of the orchestra with His golden baton. Spring is always in harmony with his performance. Spring comes to every household, leaving its calling card and inviting everyone to come out and play. The warmth of the sun is holding and embracing the universe.

The Great Ludwig van Beethoven who composed many beautiful musical numbers never heard the music of the south played in A minor. His Moonlight Sonata would have to take a back seat to the Symphony of Spring in the back woods of Arkansas.

Big Hands

For a little man who never weighed over one hundred sixty pounds, and was only 5' 4" tall, he had the hands of a "Big Man."

Those hands belong to a little man known as Ole Joe to most of his friends. A hardy handshake and a friendly slap on the back was his greeting to all his men friends. As for the women and children, he was their dad or grandpa. When those big hands, covered theirs, along with comforting words, they somehow always felt safe. The world remained upright for many with his brand of humor, often among chaos and trouble.

As for his family, he held them in the palm of those hands. As his wife and the mother of his children, I was amazed at the size of those hands and remember all the good things those hands have wrought for the children and me.

Those hands were the hands of a hard working man. They could all but envelope my hands with their size and strength. At times, those hands could be firm and harsh in certain circumstances. Yet, they were tempered with love, all for his family. Many loving deeds were also done through those hands.

How I miss the touch of those hands that were never idle until death stilled them. They were my comfort and strength in time of need. Those hands wiped many of my tears away and made things right again. I miss his hugs and the kisses we freely shared through thick and thin. Those hands that often beckoned to me, "Come go with me, mom. Let's go for a walk." Or, "Let's go to town."

Those hands worked eight hours a day to provide for the family. They played ball with the children or repaired a broken toy. Daddy's hands could do just about anything according to his kids. Ah, yes, Daddy was the man of the hour.

Those hands that were never still always worked a miracle around his household, with a gift of a coveted doll, bicycle, toy gun, or a live pony. No one but daddy could do that on a poor man's pay.

Those hands ministered to the children and me when we were sick. Both Mother and children always felt better at his soothing touch. As a minister, those hands wove harmony and good will among the sheep of his pasture, feasting on Biblical principles.

The day before he died those hands were the last thing I saw as I walked down that hospital corridor as he waved goodbye with one of those big hands. I never dreamed those hands would forever be still several hours later. Those hands would never scatter clothes, books or tools around the house anymore. Those hands are never hovering near in my hour of loneliness and grief. Those hands never reach out to pull me into his warm embrace. Those hands no longer weave happiness for me.

hose hands that were the hands of a dedicated soldier in the early part of 1940 were firm and strong when he held my hand on our wedding day. As the years passed, those hands became work worn, scarred, and wrinkled with age, a bit disfigured from a lot of wear and tear. Yet, I never saw those features in those hands. I only saw the bloom of youth and mobility etched there. Those big hands were the hands of a hero. My knight in shining armor.

Joe Riney on a picnic on Current River

What It's Like To Be Eighty

After reading George Bush's first version of what it's like to be eighty, I was prompted to write my own translation, since I passed my eightieth birthday in December 2005.

They used to call me Johnny Jump-Up, now I'm known as Johnnie Fall-Down. As the floor rises to meet me, with a goose egg on my head, some brave soul will say, "Are you hurt?"

I used to sing like a mockingbird. These days when I attempt the effort, I think there is a frog choir performing in my throat. From childhood, I've gone around the home place, day after day, whistling a happy tune. Ah, today, this old bird has even lost the pucker in my whistle.

I looked through rose-colored glasses decades ago, but today I see the world through different ones—reading and bifocals that is. I used to hear little sounds for miles around. Today I hear bells ringing in both my ears. I have a sneaking idea that's only one of life's theme songs, "Don't You Ear Those Bells Now Ringing?"

In my prime, I used to do the twist. My generation was the Jitterbug group. These days I've taken up another performing art—The St. Vitus Dance. I'll have to admit I'm pretty good at it.

Whatever happened to my shiny, sparkling hair that resembles black gold? That has changed to snow on the mountain. Perhaps that's the reason I have cold hands and feet.

Climbing a flight of stairs was once a piece of cake. I was like the little train chugging up a steep hill, saying, "I think I can, I think I can, I know I can." Now, I'm more like the little train who says, "I don't think I can, I don't think I can. I know I can't." For this old engine runs out of gas and my wheels start slipping.

My memory is a thing of the past, here today and gone tomorrow. Of all the things I've lost, I miss that the most. Memory loss has taken up the old adage, "Youth and Romance." I once could run over the hill, but now they help me over the hill. And in the romance department, well that's a zero. I used to walk over hills and plains with a spring in my step. Today I am reminded of the rabbit and the tortoise trying out for an up coming race. Like the tortoise creeping along, I get there eventually, but unlike the tortoise, I never win the race. Old club foot is my claim to fame.

I used to do a mile long sprint, with my agile off-spring, playing rough and tumble games. Today I'm lucky if I'm able to waddle across the floor, or I just might stagger through the door. My get up and go has got up and went.

Life was once a bowl of cherries, with a side dish of ice cream. Now I eat the pits and throw away the cherries. By the time I digest the pits, my ice cream has turned into rocky road soup.

Arthritis bothers me now and then; sinus is my worse enemy, always lurking around threatening to choke me. Aches and pains invade various parts of my body, which causes my joints to creak and pop. My favorite phrase is, "Oh, me."

Every morning when I crawl out of bed on all fours, muscle bound with a stiff neck, you would think Dizzy Dean had reappeared. Four or five hours later I fall back into its comfortable contours and sleep some more, while the walls vibrate with my snores.

Milk of Magnesia is a wonderful product. It puts wheels on my other-wise dragging feet. Even though I'm only a few steps from the bathroom, that's a race I can't afford to lose.

Oh, yes, I've been through the School of Hard Knocks, but I graduated with a Ph.D. (Pretty heavy Dribble). Nose dribble that is. My teacher of life presented me with a M. N. O. O. J. Bet you never heard that one. What was the occasion you ask? When I lost my teeth for some reason, it put My Nose Out of Joint. A disfigured nose sure wouldn't help my-young-at-heart image. Then and there, I decided I had enough higher learning. My biggest achievement came when I got my new prescription teeth. I actually had a mouth and I no longer had to garble my words or sing the blues.

My mind is still fairly active, but even that malfunctions now and then when I can't remember names and faces. My heart says, "you can do this or that," a dozen times a day, but my mind screams a big, "no, you can't," at every turn I make.

It gets hard to tie my shoes, brush my hair and I fumble with all the buttons on my clothes. My arms aren't long enough to pull up my zipper at the back of my dress. I wonder if that little invention called Velcro would do the trick. Oh well, I'd probably snag it open on a nail or some other obstruction, and have to face the naked truth.

My body betrays me from day to day. My knees won't bend; my arms have lost their strength. It seems as if my legs have turned to rubber and my feet to clay. I get a crick in my back and I have to rely on an old friend, Dr. Ben Gay.

This younger generation thinks we are senile, and pays us no mind. Come on down to our level and listen a spell, you might well learn a few valuable lessons from Grandma and Grandpa. If you modern hep-cats, wearing low cut jeans, and belly exposed torso, which gets their lingo from a mouse-swinging computer, would stop talking so fast and far out, we just might catch your drift. With your help—perhaps us old timers as you call us might become hep-cat swinging senior citizens. You will have to admit we deserve that well earned right.

I once had a pretty figure eight; darn if that hasn't spread all out of shape. What ever happened to my smooth clear complexion? Looking into the mirror, I see a lot of pretty lines and wrinkles spread out all over my face and arms. Oh, I just call 'em my beauty stripes or my daily make-up. Weep your heart out, you baby face gals, for the only place you can purchase this product is at a natural store. It's advertised primarily for the elderly. The store's beauty consultant promises it won't wear off. Wow, what an amazing product. You gal's who lie under a tanning bed, don't have a thing on us older generation.

I guess life isn't too bad, for when I want to dress up and look pretty; I get a new flaming tattoo, mostly reds and blues, my favorite colors that blends in nicely with all the colors I wear in my clothes. However, I guess even that has its down side, for after a few days those same acrylic paintings fade into a sickly yellow green.

Being a blood donor, I donate my blood at least once a month and I don't have to visit my Doctor over eight or ten times a year. My weight stays about the same year round.

I drool in my sleep, wear comfortable shoes on my feet. I have a hump in my back, my hearing is shot to pieces and I more than likely say yes when I should say no. Or no when I should say yes. I say I forgot many more times than I say, oh, yes, I remember.

All you Octogenarians out there take heart for when we get to the end of life's race, we are going to hear the angel's proclaim, "Would you look at all those Johnny-Jump-Ups parading around, wearing a robe and crown. They're sporting wings no less, and blowing their own horn, announcing Heaven's Jubilee.

We won't have any need for wheels as we won't have any trouble climbing those Golden Stairs. Even all our aches and pains will vanish. Laughter and happiness will be our gain. And such singing you will hear, twill be glorious, I do declare. And God's own son will be the leading one at that meeting in the air.

In the meantime, have someone load up your walker and wheelchairs, come on to my house and we'll have a time reminiscing about once upon a time and singing Auld Lang Syne.

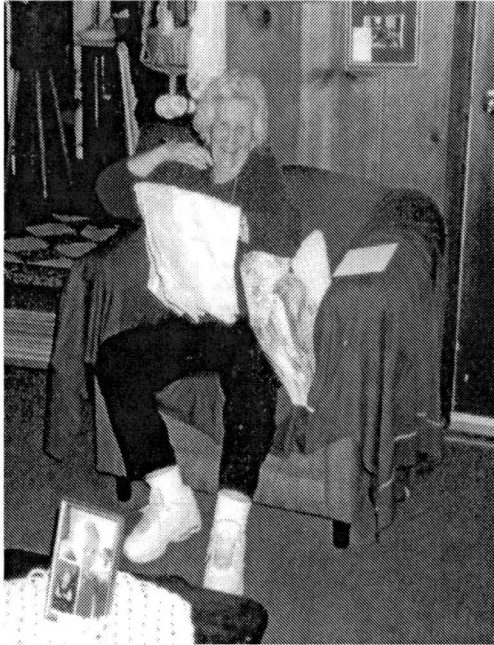

Euple's birthday party

Rain

I view the swirling clouds—
I hear the rolling thunder.
Not a breath of air is stirring—
The day is dark and somber.
Fearful lightning spears flaunts itself across the sky
like sizzling jagged, blazing veins of fire.
'Tis God's mighty hand of Power
Rain brings a multitude of pretty flowers.

Rain cascades down my windowpane
With its silvery gleam, and noisy musical refrain.
Leaving behind dirty splotches and untidy stains.
Wavy patterns make rivulets on my windows, hanging
resembling tiny streams and silver strings a dangling.

Broken clouds, the blue sky appearing,
fast the rain is disappearing
How could I be fearing when on God's picture book I was
    peering?
Beauty had spread its mantle round like tiny diamonds falling
    down.
Rain drops falling off the eaves, and dripping off the silent
    trees,
covering the water soaked ground.

Alas! the birds appearing with wet drooping wings—
while setting on a fence post or perched in a tree high in the
    sky,
preening and fluffing their feathers dry.
Their home the open sky or in an open nest nearby.
Yet their song rises high in the air on peals of ecstacy.
Fancy hearing a bird cry?

Then stealing over the land comes the bright rays of the sun.
Again 'tis God's hand waving over the earth his magic wand.
A rainbow spread its beauty out for all to see,
Showing off its many colors of pink, yellow, green and blue

its charm more intoxicating than any sweet wine an awesome
    view,
radiating with life in every circle and Technicolor hue.

Unlike the rainbow, God's promise never disappears.
It's always there, always flowing, always showing
all knowing, freely given.
His love is undying.

Beans, Potatoes and Cornbread

Breakfast at our house in the 1930's was a meal that would stick to one's ribs. Fat homemade biscuits and thickening gravy, sorghum molasses mixed with butter finished off the meal. Those molasses were cooked to a golden sheen that was extracted from the juice of sorghum cane when it was ready to harvest in the early fall. Molasses making day was a day for all the neighbors to pool their cane together and meet at the boss's house (for he was the only one who had a sorghum mill). It was not only a work day, it was also a fun day for adults and children as well, as we watched that huge bubbling cauldron of juice turn into a sweet, savory treat. All of those farm families went away with gallons of that sweet confection to make into cakes, cookies, popcorn balls, or candy. If there wasn't something else sweet on the table, it was eaten for dessert.

Taffy pulling parties were often held at someone's house. Those molasses were cooked down to a slow boil to a certain temperature then set aside to cool. Couples all over the house would pull a gob of that gooey stuff to a golden yellow, then cut it into bite size pieces. Talk about good. That was a good excuse for courting boys and girls to steal a sweet sticky kiss. Romantic dreams haunted their sleep the rest of the night.

Most of us were too poor to afford a cow for milk and butter. Our landlord was generous to share with us, until the old cow went dry. It was along about that time when imitation butter hit the grocery shelves. It came in a one pound white block along with a small package of yellow powdered food coloring. Mixing those two ingredients together, that block of white spread became a gob of yellow gold. Mighty tasty on a hot biscuit or stirred into a big spoon of jelly or molasses. Blackberry jam, plum jelly or dried peaches set on the table for those who didn't like 'lasses. That was the beginning of margarine in a tub of "I can't Believe it's not Butter."

Our noon meal (dinnertime) consisted of beans, potatoes, and cornbread. To spice up our evening meal (suppertime) we had corn bread, beans and potatoes. There was always those ever lasting molasses for dessert. Once or twice a week there was a big old yellow cake to tickle our taste buds. Smelling the aroma of that cake baking in a wood cook stove made it hard to wait for meal time. Eggs were a commodity that were saved for a dozen deviled eggs, cakes or pies for dinner, never eaten with breakfast. Junk food was not in our vocabulary, nor on the grocery shelves. At noon the farmers would come in from the fields sweaty and hungry. Shedding their smelly wet shirts, hats and shoes, they washed up at the outside pump before they sat down to eat a hot meal in a hot house. After an hour of rest and a few cat naps outside under a shade tree, they would don that same smelly shirt, hat and shoes and go back to the fields for a long afternoon in the blazing hot sun behind a team of plodding horses pulling a plow or cultivator. Such was the life of a farmer tilling the soil.

After washing up the dinner dishes, the women folks and the teenage girls would follow the men to the field soon after, wearing a long sleeved shirt, overalls, heavy shoes and an old straw hat or sunbonnet. Teenagers were not running up and down the road listening to a car radio or eating between meals on junk food, they worked right alongside the adults. The only time we ate what could be considered junk food was once a week when we went to town, we may have had ice cream in a cone, soda pop, or a bar of candy. "Bit o Honey" was my favorite candy bar, that chewy bit of taffy satisfied my sweet tooth. Then there was the Baby Ruth, the Milky Way and the Three Musketeers. Orange and grape soda, RC colas, Pepsi, and Coke was the most sought after drink. In fact, there wasn't much choice other than those six flavors. I am reminded of a popular song us teenagers use to sing while drinking our coke in a little hole in the wall called a café—"Drinking Rum and Coca Cola." Who needed rum when we had a bag of roasted peanuts to munch along with our Coke. That little hole in the wall was a hangout for dozens of teenagers as we listened to our favorite songs, belted from a blaring juke box on a Saturday afternoon, while flirting and making goo-goo eyes at the opposite sex.

A young fryer chicken killed, plucked, gutted and washed, cut up and then cooked in an iron skillet to a crispy brown for Sunday dinner, was a delicious treat. Potatoes and chicken gravy with all of the essence of those crispy chicken crumbs was far better than just plain gravy made out of a little grease, flour and milk. Biscuits always went with chicken. Sliced bread didn't come until years later. The old red rooster was sacrificed to make chicken and dumplings or dressing. Ah, yes, eating those meals were like eating steak cooked on a grill.

My dad was a fisherman who kept us supplied with fish practically year round. Those crispy gold nuggets cooked in lard, was a fisherman's dream. Four or five big old bullfrogs became a supper of fried frog legs. They were a delicacy. Sinking them into a pot of hot grease, they began to quiver and jump. A young child seeing those limbs come alive was a little nerve racking. But it never affected the taste when it came time to eat them.

There was no such thing as turkey and dressing in those days. The only time I ever saw a turkey was a picture in a book or magazine. (Later my husband and I raised turkeys.) What a difference a turkey made. We ate turkey and dressing with all the trimmings, along with the rest of the nation, baked in a gas or electric oven. Even though we ate our feast out of Five-and-Dime store plates, it was just as good as it was eaten off the finest china.

Unless one is old as seventy or eighty years, you probably never ate any crackin' bread. It was made from the fat of a corn fed pig. All the fat was trimmed from it to be cooked into lard in a big pot outside till those little brown gobs of fat would be a crispy golden brown, ready to put in a bowl of cornmeal, flour and milk to make cracklin' bread fresh from the oven. It was a meal in itself. (Don't knock it if you have never had any.) Fish, frog legs, cornbread or cracklin' bread seemed to go together and was a fine meal at anyone's table. (Hush puppies had not been dreamed up.)

Seventy years later, I am also reminded of a frosty winter morning and slices of ham and sausage sizzling in an iron skillet on a wood stove with red gravy and a big fat biscuit to sop up its goodness. Icicles a foot long might be hanging from the eve of the house, but we were toasty and warm inside our home, the children eating those icicles minus the flavor were like my grandchildren eating a flavorful Popsicle today.

I betcha you never smoked any rabbit tobacco either. Rabbit tobacco grew wild around our place. When the leaves dried up a couple of my friends and I would crush those dried leaves into powder and roll us a hefty cigarette. There were always matches and cigarette papers lying around a smoker's house. We were careful not to get caught snitching them. Hiding out behind the barn, we enjoyed a few stolen moments of crime, right under my family's nose. Puffing and blowing we savored our hour of sin.

Woven around eight decades of my life are times I shall never forget. For me we've lived the good life. City lights thousands of miles away, with all its glitz and glamour and famous restaurants did not have a thing on us "pore country folk."

Sweet Mama and the Dive

A dive was a place of ill repute.

In 1934 and 1935, my daddy was a handsome man who loved to dress in his Sunday best, every bit the man about town. There weren't too many men that could compete with my dad; for looks or immaculate dress.

In my first book, *Reflections*, I wrote about the Good Life, but this little episode touched our lives for a period of time on the steamy side when my daddy found a girlfriend. Daddy had been a widower for several years at this time and he was lonely. People, including women, who frequently hit a well-known seedy dive in town did not fit in decent folk's society. They wasted no time on such places, or the people who went there. Brawling and fighting, booze flying freely, dancing the night away were common occurrences, not to mention flying knives or a bottle broken over someone's head. That was the way of life on a Saturday night. It was considered to be a den of iniquity, sinners and loose women.

This is where my daddy found his Sweet Mama. Sweet Mama was a misnomer for never would she be our Sweet Mama. Many of the women who went to this place of ill repute had a nickname—names such as Leaping Lena, Weeping Mary, and Toe Tapping Jane. What a sorrowful sad life some of those women and men lived just for another drink. The women were forever trying to con some man out of another drink or a few pennies.

Not being a drinking man, daddy started going there for the love of dancing, and was captured by a pair of pretty eyes. (To this day, I do not remember her real name.) We kept our distance between her and her family, my sister at home resented every outing daddy made to her house and the hard earned money he gave to her and her two pretty teenage daughters. They were following in their Mama's footsteps.

Daddy's girlfriend had a husband that encouraged her and daddy's dates. That was one more reason for the resentment and dislike. It could all be summed up in my sister's eyes—daddy had lost his mind.

I was nine-years-old the day I remember so well, when those two pretty daughters who wore the prettiest clothes, wearing expensive rouge, lipstick and eye shadow came by our house. They were actually driving a car! Women driving cars in those days were almost nil. They touched our lives, or I should say mine. I thought those young girls were beautiful, wearing their finery and all their make-up. Pulling up in front of our little house, they asked me to go with them, to show them the field where daddy was working. For some reason, Sis was not at home at the time, but we lived a stones throw of our neighbors. In my childish mind, not knowing the repercussions it would bring, I got in the car with those up-town girls and gloried in their presence. I never did know what they wanted with my dad, for they left me sitting in the car. Probably money, for daddy was a sucker for a pretty face.

As we pulled up to the house some thirty minutes later, my sister came boiling out of that house like a thousand angry bees bent on mayhem, breathing fire and brimstone. She didn't know but what someone had kidnapped me. She jerked that car door open with such vengeance—it scared those girls half to death. She gave them a tongue lashing I bet they never forgot.

"What do you mean taking my little sister off with you? Don't you ever, and I stress, ever come back here again or set your feet anywhere near here again," she said. "If you do, I'll beat you within an inch of your life." She could have done it too, mad as she was and besides she was bigger than they were. Young and innocent as I was, I couldn't understand why she was so angry with those girls when I was the guilty party by running away from home without her permission.

My daddy's fling ended on the wild side of life after almost two years, when someone almost stuck a knife in his ribs one night at the notorious dive. Another man saw what was happening and kicked the knife away. That was a revelation for dad. He realized he was playing with fire and his life.

Such were the hard facts of life he learned, almost losing his life on that party filled summer night. That was his last and final fling on the Steamy Side of Life. Daddy's dancing days were over. He never strayed from the straight and narrow again. As far as I was concerned, it was my first lesson in crime. Not to be lured into a car by good-looking, sweet talking girls.

The First Time I Saw You

The first time I saw you, bells went off in my head. Fireworks flared and rained down all around us. Birds sang a sweeter song that echoed inside my beating heart. Stars glowed brighter across the galaxy of my universe. Angel music plucked at my heart strings while I sang a romantic melody.

The first time I saw you, your voice spoke volumes to me. I was mesmerized with expectation and ties that bind. I saw a promise mirrored in the depth of shining hazel eyes that left a reflection of a caricature of my own image. I caught a glimpse of the future, a vision.

I began to hear wedding bells in the recesses of my mind. I almost spoke aloud in my fantasy—"I do." Babies were conjured up. Enchantment walking beside me. I believe I saw five of them, soft and cuddly with hazel eyes. From deep within my happy heart, I heard the joy and laughter of babies, small children, and handsome teenagers. Some of them would look like you and the rest like me. Young as I was—just fifteen, I couldn't conjure up grandchildren, nor great grandchildren sixty years later.

All of a sudden I was reminded life is just a vapor—here today and gone tomorrow. Wedding bells did ring four years later, five babies were born who soon grew up and moved away. Father Time taught me a lesson—reality is often harsh, tempered with determination and hard work. Yet sweetened by love and respect. For forty-seven years that star struck fifteen-year-old girl's dream became much more than she could ever imagine the first time she saw you.

Standing by your hospital bed one cold December day in 1991, my hands enveloped in your work scarred hands, we shared the magic again as we kissed good-bye, expecting to see each other the next visiting day. We never dreamed that was to be the last time I saw you.

A happy smile, a lingering kiss, a hasty good-bye with a wave of your hand followed me down that long hospital corridor, having high hopes you would be home in a few days.

That hope was shattered when death robbed me, leaving me desolate. The magic and enchantment I dreamed of so long ago was gone. The companionship and the relationship that belonged to only you and I—today and tomorrow faded from my view as I sobbed out my grief and despair.

The strong voice that had always steered the course of the family's lives faded away into the dawn of a new day, down the corridor of heaven with a wave of the hand and a whispered farewell.

One day in the near future, our voices will blend again. Once more, I can say, "The first time I saw you." Where angelic music will not be a fantasy, a foolish teenager's dream following us from the first time I saw you.

A Nostalgic Look into the Past

"Soap operas" were never heard of before the arrival of television. They were simply called, "The Stories." Day and night radio was our biggest entertainment of the 1940's. Once in a blue moon we went to the show house to see a movie. My sister, sister-in-law and I would gather around the radio every Monday thru Friday to listen to *Stella Dallas, Helen Trent, Ma Perkins*, and others, but those three were our favorites. *Ma Perkins* was the matriarch of a large family who was a grandmother, friend, teacher, counselor, nursemaid, and one the whole family looked to for advice and companionship. Now *Helen Trent* and *Stella Dallas* were Hollywood material all wrapped up in glamour and their many love lives. Ah, yes, they brought a little glamour and excitement to our own simple lives. They became real people, as we got so engrossed in their lives of mystery and intrigue. *All My Children* and *General Hospital*, today's soap operas fade in comparison to those old stories six decades ago.

Television was only a figment of someone's imagination when I was a child. There was talk of a radio being invented with a screen like a movie screen, where one could see people and places all over the United States. I could not imagine in my childish mind how that could be possible. Many years went by before it became a reality. Radio somehow faded into the background when "The Stories" became "Soap Operas" and familiar faces danced across a screen. (Black and white was the early versions.) Not since the automobile was ever such an invention received with such approval and astonishment.

On Saturday night from eight o'clock to midnight, *The Grand Ole Opry* performed from the Ryman Auditorium in Nashville, Tennessee (1885-2004). Musicians, singers and comedians came from all over the U. S. with their brand of humor and musical talent. Uncle Dave Macon was the MC for many years. His booming voice opened the show with a huge welcome to the Grand Ole Opry that brought down the house and the fun began.

The old rafters on our house rang with the sound of music and laughter. It was the best, and families all across the country never missed a performance. Roy Acuff would open up on that old harmonica and you could hear that "Wabash Cannonball's" lonesome whistle whine and hear that engine growling and rumbling down that old railroad track.

Then there was Hank Williams, *Jambalaya* and crawfish pie, *I'm So Lonesome I Could Cry,* was on the top chart list for many months. Even though a lot of people had never eaten jambalaya, when one heard Hank sing, their taste buds came alive. Ernest Tubb made the tear jerker, *Walking the Floor Over You* famous. Johnny Cash, the man in black, warbled through *Folsom Prison Blues.* He could make you feel that the tug of those prison gates were not for you. Johnny and his wife, June Carter, often sang together. Before Johnny came along, it was the Carter Family and Mother Maybelle.

Bob Wills and his Texas Playboys strummed out, *The Yellow Rose of Texas,* and *San Antonio Rose,* in harmony with the fragrance of a yellow rose. Red Foley, Hank Snow, Porter Wagoner, The Wilburn Family, Flatt & Scruggs, Bill Monroe, Patsy Cline, Loretta Lynn, Kitty Wells, Cowboy Copas, Buck Owens, and his Buckaroos, Little Jimmy Dickens, Faron Young, the Rhodes Family, and many others made the Grand Ole Opry famous.

We must not forget the funny people. Minnie Pearl with her little girl clothes and the store bought hat with the tag still attached, wearing bows on her shoes was a bit of sunshine, as her "HOW-DEE," rang out over the airwaves. Her imaginary family from Grinder's Switch came to life. Uncle Nabob and Brother got the biggest share.

String Bean rightly got his name as he was tall and skinny. He always wore patches on his clothes. Grandpa Jones wore a rumpled hat, clothes too big for him and a pair of rubber knee boots, as did Lonzo and Oscar. They all kept us in stitches. *Amos and Andy* made their appearance on the Grand Ole Opry every so often. They portrayed themselves as hobos with their toes coming out of their shoes, and their hair protruding from a torn cap, settling somewhat off center. Amos and Andy held their own show in the late afternoon. So did *Lum and Abner.* The telephone at the beginning of the show would ring, most of the time it would be Lum who would answer and say, "Jot-em-down-store. This is Lum speaking, can I help you?" Sometimes it would be their crony known as Kingfisher. *Amos and Andy, Lum and Abner* were a must that we couldn't miss. Red Skelton was our favorite nighttime show. Red's Clem Kadiddlehopper and Freddy the Freeloader and his little boy act stole the show. Then there was George Burns and Gracie Allen. *Fibber McGee and Molly*, and ah, *The Lone Ranger* and his Indian sidekick Tonto. There never was any doubt the bad guys got their due when the Lone Ranger, sitting astride his rearing horse, ended the show with "Hi-Ho-Silver, away!" *Tarzan of the Apes* sent chills down my back as he made the call of the wild, swinging through the trees, wearing only a leopard skin. After the wild kingdom was restored, he had the lovely Jane to come home to.

Sitting around a cozy wood fire on a winter's night, with coffee brewing on the stove with a bowl of popcorn fresh from an iron skillet, our home had the appearance of the *Twilight Zone* as a feeble kerosene lamp gave out its light and shadows.

To the few who remember the era of radio as we knew it in the '30's and '40's, it was the sum of wholesome entertainment, a forgotten melody only a few can sing today.

The Grand Canyon

Standing on the rim of the Grand Canyon in the spring of 2005, looking out over that panoramic, awesome, inspiring abyss of cliffs, sun washed with fire, I heard what could only be called angelic music from the "Portals of Heaven." Gently rocking me in the cradle of freedom's song. Yet, it played havoc with my emotions, and tugged at my heart strings.

Looking deeply into the canyon's mysterious looking glass, I fancied I saw the image of my lost love and heard him say, *Drink to me only with thine eyes, and I will pledge with mine, or leave a kiss within the cup, and I'll not ask for wine. The thirst that from the soul doth rise, doth ask a drink divine, But might I of Jove's nectar sip. I would not change for thine.* Taken from the old forgotten lovely ballad written in 1616 by a Elizabethan poet known as Ben Johnson.

Like a young bride, I whispered yes! Seeking my lost youth, I was haunted by love's old sweet song. Every sip I took along that historical path was set to music of a divine operetta. The stage was set and played out in three acts entitled, "The Big, The Bold, and The Beautiful.

Accolades of praise from hundreds of spectators as the curtain came down on another grand performance. Shouts of "Bravo" could be heard rolling over that huge amphitheater. It's audience enthralled with the one of a kind show. Captivated with those magnificent marbled cliffs and temple-like pinnacles of rock and stone, I was amazed at such splendor rising thousands of feet into the atmosphere, whose kingdom covers two hundred and seventy-seven miles (according to the *National Geographic*) with the mighty Colorado River running through it. It is a breathtaking, mind-boggling scene that has baffled scores of explorers and scientific minds. Numbered with the stars of heaven, it's hard for a lowly human being to comprehend its significance, or the feeling of humbleness one gets among those enormous moss covered cathedrals of nobility and elegance. A gospel song kept running through my mind, and I was found wanting. *The Rock That is Higher Than I.* O, then to the rock let me fly, like an art critic trying to evaluate a priceless painting. The Grand

32

Canyon—a priceless gem is truly the workmanship of an artistic genius. A Rembrandt or a Van Gogh would fade in comparison.

Soaking up that miraculous tableau spread out before me, time seemed to stand still as I drifted away into the realms of an unknown world where romance, mystery and intrigue is forever locked away in that cavernous mouth. Lost in the pages of history, I held a huge volume of knowledge in my hands; I could never compete nor understand. Only the Divine Interpreter can unlock its mystery. However, fantasy's teacher opened the door and I became her willing scholar.

Those mighty columns and peaks rear their colossal heads out of what seemed like a bottomless pit that becomes a playground behind them for hundreds of white rolling clouds always drifting onward. Like children playing hide and seek, they skip across the endless clear cobalt blue sky, painted by the Master's Hand. Soon tiring of their game, they hide themselves in infinity's garden to be seen no more. However, the game goes on as others take their place.

Straggling rain clouds often follow in their wake, bringing a spring shower. A rainbow heightens the canyon's beauty as it arches its way across elegant sculptured movements of grandeur and finesse. An eagle soaring overhead adds to the drama and mystery of that mighty gorge. One can't help but wonder how it was molded and shaped into what one sees today.

They that wait upon the Lord shall renew their strength, they shall mount up with wings of an eagle, they shall run and not be weary, they shall walk and not faint. Isa: 40:31. Anyone who has ever seen this giant painting of poetry come to life never goes away without feeling they have discovered something scared and holy. No will one ever forget its beauty or the magnitude of its surroundings. The voice of God seems to echo across its boundaries as He proclaims, "It is good."

Ah, yes, the Grand Canyon (rightly named) is a place of wonder and disbelief. It is a place to love. It is a place to listen to its melody of songs and hear music, to learn to question its rightful place in the annuals of antiquity.

It is truly an oasis of friendly giants and towering citadels for hungry, thirsty souls. On entering its vast portals of elegance and open door policy, it loudly shouts welcome. Partaking of its repast, I felt a sense of completion, sustaining my own hungry, thirsty soul. Ambrosia, the food of royalty, was set before me and I ate lavishly of its manna. Drinking it all in—reeling with the wonder of it all, I became intoxicated while sipping from the cup of immortality. Conversing with ghosts of a lost generation, the drum rolled with sound and fury. The wind of change and the echo of an enduring era. Yet the canyon holds secrets it will never tell, hidden under layers of sediment and tons of monolithic rock formations. Where else can one find the miracle of the loaves and the fishes multiplied a hundred-fold by the culinary skills of an expert connoisseur in action? Surely my cup runnth over.

On leaving the park at days end, I felt the spirit of adventure and the lure of wooded trails that left a lasting impression of a living, breathing tapestry of nature framed by invisible hands, where the open sky and the stars are the summit of the city where the Son is the light.

A writer once described this marvel of creation as "The vault of Heaven." Bathed in flaming Technicolor, it is an artist's unfurled canvas and a photographer's dream. A scene of a mule train hundreds of feet below looked like a miniature carousal in slow motion.

The canyon tells a different story to each and every individual. As for me, I heard sweet music from a divine source, and I poured out my soul with the symphony of heaven. The wings of the wind brought the drum beat of a rain dance and I felt the ground vibrate under my feet. I heard an unfinished composition written for me and I cried. Yet I felt a caress holding me gently in its embrace, enfolding me like a warm blanket. Standing there listening to nature's song, I felt a kinship with the wild and free, higher and higher I fled to a haven of rest. In gratitude, I uttered the words of a song *My God How Great Thou Art*, while witnessing a miracle on a wind-swept mountain pass near Flagstaff, Arizona.

Perhaps it can be summed up by John Greenleaf Whitter's moving ballad that awoke the sleeping poet within me as I recalled these beautiful opening lines that also expressed my own sentiments.

One hymn more, O my lyre!

Praise to the God above,
of Joy and life and love
Sweeping its strings of fire!

Dedicated to my two oldest daughters, Rhonda and Regina, who supported me and walked me through that magical kingdom. My heartfelt thanks are not enough for what I received in exchange. Unlike the slightly handicapped mother and grandmother, I was Dorothy in Oz, skipping down the yellow brick road.

Rhonda and Mom

Overlooking the Grand Canyon

You Better Watch Out or the Ol' Booger-Man Will Get You

That was the refrain I often heard as a child, when I was naughty. We were taught not to lie, say bad words, or misbehave, especially in the presence of others. If a child was caught stealing, that was an ultimate crime—punishable by a peach tree switch. One wore his or her prison stripes for a whole day in mortal disgrace.

Falling down in the floor, kicking and screaming with a mad fit simply was not tolerated but once or twice. A big hand was applied in a blistering sting. A child remembered the next time they were tempted. I tried that one on for size one day, when my sister was busy in the kitchen. She told me to put some wood in the kitchen stove. I refused. Then the trouble began as Sis tried to make me do it by applying a few light taps on my bottom—just enough to make me mad. Falling down in the floor, I was having a royal fit. My big brother came through the kitchen at that moment and saw what was happening. He never said a word as he slowly took off his belt. One stinging lick and then another as that belt cracked across my backside. The results were two goose-eggs that popped up immediately on my exposed flesh, and I thought I was on fire. I was sure he had branded me with two red hot coals from that old hot stove. Scrambling up from the wooden floor as fast as I could, I ran to the fire box and the blocks of wood nearby, where I wasted no time in getting wood in that stove. All I could think of was escaping that blistering strap. Screaming at the top of my lungs, blubbering tears and snot, I said, "I'll put it in. I'll put it in." Believe me; I did it in record time, too.

I think my brother was a little ashamed he had to give me a licking for I don't recall he ever hit me again. Yet he made a believer out of me. From then on, when he said jump—I jumped. As soon as I could, I slunk away in helpless fury, vowing to myself, of course, I'd hate them both forever.

Threatening me with the ol' booger-man didn't help either. He was a mixture of everything bad, with his bloodshot eyes, complete with horns and a pitchfork, laughing his evil head off at

36

my expense when I had misbehaved. I guess I heard my sister say, "The ol' Booger-Man will get you for that," two or three times a day.

Seems like I was always waiting for the ax to fall. The capricious child that I was, the threat was always hanging over my head. If I told a whopper, and got away with it, guilt in the shape of a horned monster stood by my bedside all night as I tossed and turned. The only way I could get away from him was to pull the covers up over my head and cower in fright, sure he would get me before morning. Even then I believed I could feel the prick of his pitchfork. Fueling the fires of the Bad Place (one didn't say H___ either), burning my feet all night. Not until the sun brightened up the room the next morning, did I realize the Booger-Man hadn't got me after all. He always disappeared at the dawning of the day and I was safe, at least until the next time when I heard Sis say, "The ol' Booger-Man will get you!" For me the ol' Booger-Man was a nightmare come true.

Take for instance the time my cousin Mary and I, as small children, went on a crime spree, then told a cock-and-bull story about where we had gotten our loot. (We got away with it too.) Committing two crimes in one day was a little disturbing to say the least. Ignoring any little nagging doubts we had, we entered the Five and Dime, keeping a sharp eye out for the clerks. We loaded our pockets with balloons in all colors of the rainbow, little balloons, big balloons, and in betweens. Escaping on foot, we figured we had pulled off a successful robbery with our slight of hand. We were pretty proud of our accomplishment as we blew them up one after the other, over and over, sailing them through the air on pieces of string. After hours of fun our bubbles began to burst into the blackness of night when it came time to go to bed.

Whispering and giggling, we reviewed our fun day and boldly planned another robbery the next day. It had been so easy. We were on our way to fame and fortune. (Little did I know.) Finally drifting off to sleep, dreams began to haunt me and I heard the voice of my sister, "The ol' Booger-Man is going to get you this time for sure." One crime was bad enough, but two! There was no alibi for being a liar and a thief. Coming up from the fires of forever, I saw the ol' Booger-Man posed and ready.

There was no escape—trapped and doomed, I heard his evil laughter and felt his hot breath on my face. Gasping for breath, I threw up my hands in desperation, crying, "No, no, I'll never tell another lie or steal anything ever again!"

Suddenly the light of day came bursting through and I was free. I lost a part of my childhood and the Booger-Man's image faded. I learned a very valuable lesson for my sister was never able to frighten me from that day on with, "The ol' Booger-Man will get you!"

A Dear John Letter

Dear John:

Please release me of the promise to marry you. I have since changed my mind. I want to be free to date other guys. Hope you understand. Sincerely,

How could a young man far from home fighting for the cause of freedom, possibly giving his life to protect his loved ones back home, except and understand those cruel words?

That was the gist of the letter I sent to the man I had promised to marry during WWII. There were hundreds of those young men who got those Dear John letters, while the girl got off scot-free to play the field elsewhere. It made little difference if they broke the soldier's heart. Many of us girls were more in love with the uniform than the man who wore it. A girl had clout if she was engaged to a soldier, sailor or Marine. She savored her power over the girls who didn't have a uniform man. There was something special in those made-to-order uniforms that appealed to the eye that made all the girls swoon and fall in love overnight.

Unless a girl was a WAVE or a WAC the war didn't affect young girls too much, for news was often days behind before it reached the home front. Censured letters that came through never told very much. One day your man was in Germany, France, or perhaps Holland, and the next day, he would be in some other unknown country.

How fickle and unthoughtful we young girls were, in that war torn period of our lives. Many of those boys died holding their sweetheart's picture, and letters close to their heart. Those pictures made us aware of the conflicts of war for awhile, but then the glamour of good looking soldier boys from all walks of life coming to our town almost daily, filled our lives completely. We sang such patriotic songs, like *The Battle Hymn of the Republic*, *The Star Spangled Banner*, *America the Beautiful*, pledging our alligence to the flag, our God and country.

I wonder if God wasn't a little bit put out with us smug, carefree young women, parading around in our best bib and tucker, while a lot of those boys were holed up in a foxhole—

cold and hungry, scared half to death in a war torn country in a foreign land.

Getting back to my Dear John. I met him before the war when I was a senior in a little country school known as Hamil. He was in his middle twenties, over six feet tall with a physique other boys would die for. One that all the girls drooled over. He was every girl's dream with a heart catching smile that matched his outgoing personality. He was the envy of my group of girlfriends, and I ate it all up while hanging on his strong arm. An added attraction was his car.

Not many boys had their own car in the forties. When I saw that little black, shiny A-Model Ford Coupe, complete with a rumble seat, chugging down our country road, I knew he was coming to my house. Running to the mirror, I powered and perfumed and ran a comb through my long black hair, before I went out to meet him.

Our romance, such as it was, included going to the movies every now and then, a church social, a picnic with friends, or a ball game. Our dates never come to anything serious until the war came along. War, however, paints a different picture in the hearts and lives of the young. John was handsome before he donned that uniform but afterwards he was a big WOW! I couldn't take my eyes off him. I believed at the time I could follow him to the ends of the earth when he asked me to wait for him just before he went overseas. That was a promise I never kept. Later, I realized as a sixteen-year-old, I was not ready to make that commitment. That was what prompted the Dear John letter.

From the beginning, our friendship was just a boy and a girl thing—who were attracted to each other and had fun together. There were never rockets exploding between us, no bells ringing, stars shining brighter, or a merry-go-round we hoped would never stop.

We were comfortable with each other until the war put a different perspective on our decision to live a single life, or get married. War brides and sweethearts were a dime a dozen in almost every household in America.

Two years later, I met and married another soldier boy, who became my soul mate for forty-seven years, and the father of our five children. Only then did I realize why I didn't have those overpowering lifetime feelings for my Dear John.

By this time you are wondering what happened to John (not his real name). The old cliché, "stranger than fiction," often follows our destiny. In the early days of our dating days, John was dating my eighth-grade schoolteacher in between our dates. I was more than a little awed of her, and a mite jealous, for she was everything I was not. Tall and slim, very pretty, older and educated, she wore tailor-made suits and hats, with the latest footwear, compared to my plain homemade creations. She looked like a fashion model from the big city. I'll have to admit; I gloated a bit after he stopped seeing her, and chose me over the pretty teacher. John came home safe and sound after the war was over and married that same teacher.

Even though I was a little envious of my childhood teacher, I shall always have fond memories of Miss Chester—who was the backbone and the inspiration of a small country school in the hills of Arkansas. As far as John, he was more like a big brother, who respected and protected me from the trials of life? He was a gentleman of the highest caliber and for that I say, "Thank you, Dear John." Part of my youth became a forgotten era with the passing away of time.

When my beloved G. I. Joe passed away, it was much worse than giving him up to war. Images of the war he helped to fight often plagued his mind and he was finally put to rest December 11, 1991.

Cheers to my one and only G. I. Joe—who has finally reached his beloved Homeland riding on a ship known as Old Faithful. Bonjour, my love.

Sing Me A Song

Sing me a song of love, and laughter,
over flowing into a goblet of sweet wine
ever after.

Sing me a song of pretty flowers
and a spring rain
Rain drops kissing tiny petals with
fragrance along the garden lane.

Sing me a song of lullabies and babies
Nestled in a mother's embrace
love child without any mights or maybes.

Sing me a song of trees and a gurgling brook
Twisting and swirling its silver frock
along a shady nook.

Sing me a song of kisses and hugs
me and my baby will do the jitterbug
while cutting a rug

Sing me a song of clear blue skies, and
a multi-colored rainbow
Spreading out magical garment across Heaven's
after glow.

Sing me a song of wonder and delight
Touched by angels and sing me a song
of a cup of sweet wine.

Sing me a song of a sweet refrain.

Sing me a song of wedded bliss,
Sheltered somewhere in between a
little Mr. and a tiny Miss.

A Sequel to the Old Woods Road

Since 1947 and 1948, and the early part of 1949, we built our house adjacent to the old woods road. I've looked out my living room window all these years and remembered those early years we passed through it, my family and I in a rubber tired wagon, pulled by Bill and Tobe, our two mules.

The back half, behind our home today stretched across the back forty of our place, long overgrown with brush. The front half, always a daily reminder, is still there, overgrown as well. But so full of memories.

In the summer of 2006, I heard the whine of chain saws, and saw the devastation of the beautiful trees along the borders of its tree-lined avenue and beyond. Huge bulldozers and gas guzzling monsters called a log loader, invaded its beauty, cutting, slashing and loading a truck with hundreds of those huge logs.

As my mind traveled backward, I am reminded there were no chainsaws, nor thousand pounds of heavy equipment in the woods in the 1940's. There were only crosscut saws, men, powerful mules or horses.

I brush tears away as I watch the activity of the workers, setting high in the seat of those giant movers, loading a huge truck with dozens of logs piled high on the bed.

The old woods road has been carved out much wider, its surface is clean of all the bushes and brambles of all the seasons that have come and gone.

Yet I see its sister road of yesterday as I hear the rumble and creak of our four wheel carriages. The slow plod of farm animals trudging across its terrain. A mother's song blending in sweetly with the choir of song birds perched high in a tree. I see a father's hand guiding the path of his two charges, as he gently slaps them on the backside with the reins he holds, as his "gittup," resounds over the hills of freedom. The chatter of two little happy boys that surely delighted their guardian angel hovering overhead. A gentle breeze capered happily through the trees, while the sun smiled down on its family of four, warming the cockles of their heart on an outing of fun and relaxation.

Yes, those mighty machines dissolved into my memory book of dreams.

If love could be exchanged for money and memories with a bagful of pocket change that small strip of road and its borderline of trees could be mine. I could have bought it for a song many times over.

The old woods road after they bulldozed it

Kerry

As a child, I loved to read fairy tales, most of the time they began with, "Once upon a time." Much later when I had children of my own, our nightly recreation was reading the classics, *Mother Goose* and the fairy tales.

In the 1950's and 1960's, a little boy came to visit our house at least once a week, sometimes over the weekend, to play with my two small boys. So I think it is appropriate I began Kerry's story with, "Once upon a time…"

Kerry was a normal sized little boy—with a million dollar smile. That smile belied the mischief gleaming in his big blue eyes. He had a rather plump little nose, ears that stuck out over his short-cropped blonde hair. Joe Louis would have been envious of Kerry's swaggering walk. That was the little neighbor boy who stole the Riney family's heart with his happy-go-lucky smile. I shall always carry that little boy image in my heart as I watched him and our sons at play.

Weekdays before sending them off to school, with a washcloth in hand, I'd give them the once over, to be sure they were clean, and with clean clothes on. When it came Kerry's turn for inspection, I'd raise my voice five or six octaves higher and in a little girl's voice, pretending to be Little Red Riding Hood facing the Big Bad Wolf, I'd say, "What big ears you have!" That was a ritual we played out each time. He never lost his cool even when I was digging the gook out of his big ears. Clean and polished, I'd send all three of them off to school on the big yellow bus. Just before boarding the bus, they turned and waved good-bye, blowing me a kiss. Kerry never failed to tell me he had a good time, often with a kiss.

Two little boys and their playmate could conjure up all kinds of mischief. They roamed all over our eighty-acre farm. The south wind blew and lingered in their hair and three little brown sun-kissed pint-sized soldiers fought a war along with an imagery army in the open fields and among the many trees that covered a lot of the farm. Warring parties of the redskin were always slaughtered by the hundreds. "Fort Riney," was well fortified, and its stock well protected. It stood the attack well, even with deadly arrows flying through the air. Shouts of "I got

45

'em," as the white trio set their sights on half-naked screaming Indians. Then the horse patrol took over, carrying the flag of victory among the blood and carnage as the bugle brigade blew the freedom's song.

They never could explain why Kerry's blonde mane didn't fall under an Indian knife hand, for a coveted scalp. In their quiet moments they all three dreamed of being another Roy Rogers, Davy Crockett or The Lone Ranger.

Not only were horses used in time of war, they were the star of the show on the range in pursuit of rounding up the cattle, searching for a lost cow and calf. There were often rumors of cattle thieves roaming the ranch. The sheriff and his posse always got their man. Cowboy was their favorite handle, "Just call me cowboy," was their namesake. Yet no real western cowboy could compete with their expertise or outride them on a mean-eyed bronc.

In the summer months, "Play ball," could be heard across the open-field—next to the house as other friends joined the game. The open field was often a race track, buzzing with horses and jockeys, wearing Levis and checkered shirts, cowboy hats and boots as their trademarks.

The creek was a swimming pool for the boys wearing their "birthday suits." Romping and splashing with a barking dog who demanded a part of the action. Trees were a challenge to see who could climb the highest. Tall tales were told, an occasional cigarette was often confiscated (without the knowledge of the adults, of course). Cap guns and knives were traded and races were run. Torn clothing and skinned knees were often the results of a tumble.

In the wintertime, there was even more fun and laughter as they played in the snow, racing down the hill on a board. Skating on the frozen bed of the creek, or riding their favorite horses through the woods and along a country road nursing cold hands and feet. When it became too cold to linger outdoors, it never seemed to bother them when they trailed mud and melted snow across Mama's floor. Flexing muscles of seven and eight-year-olds, they often arm-wrestled to see which one was the strongest and the toughest.

All of this from three small boys, who in time grew into teenagers that gave up all the games to set their sights on the pretty girls. At this time, their dreams changed to marrying a Princess and living happily ever after. My two older girls have never forgotten a young man's smile and his winning ways. (But the girls are another story.)

Of all the boys who came to our home, Kerry, was the favorite playmate and buddy. As an adopted son, he fit right into our family circle. One word was special—when he forgot and called me Mama. I carry a picture in my heart as I remember three little, often noisy, grubby-faced boys, who did their daring exploits all across the stage of life.

It is with regret that little boy grew up and moved to the "Big City," many miles away. Kerry, seeing you once a year isn't nearly enough. The family has missed you, cowboy.

My sentiments goes out to a little neighbor boy (who will always be a little boy to me), who was much more than just a neighbor to the Riney family.

Dreams do come, true for all three married their fairy-tale Princess and have lived happily ever after.

Keep smiling, Kerry, but keep your ears clean!

Love you, Cowboy.

What is a Mother?

Mothers come in several colors and many sizes. She may be a teenager or a senior citizen. She may speak one of the many languages of the world, but to her child it is the language of love. Mothers are found wherever you go. She is as common as apple pie and baseball. Yet she sits as Queen in her household. She may live in a mansion on Park Avenue, or in an humble cottage by the side of the road, yet they have one thing in common. "Motherhood." No one else can run her household as well as she. She is beauty in the kitchen, wearing a plain comfortable garment with her hair up in rollers and up to her elbows in flour with a streak of flour across her nose and forehead, baking cookies for her family. No one in all the whole wide world can cook like Mama.

Her first prerogative is being a mother, but on the other hand, she is a friend, a buddy, a companion, a teacher, a counselor, a nurse and often a miracle worker. All she has to do is give out a hug or kiss, whispering comforting words in her children's ear that will cure just about any problem. Yet her children often think of her as a jailor, a warden, a truant officer, and a mind reader. It is hard to escape the probing eyes in the back of her head.

To her, ten thousand words can't compare to that one word, "Mama." Nor will she ever experience a greater thrill than when her children give her a big hug and kiss, simply because they love her. They are bound by a love that only mother and child can know. Even if she knows her children are wrong, she will love them regardless of whatever they have done. That technology is called love's strong cord. Mother would lay down her life for her off-spring if she could, and would never regret it to the very end. No other person will work as much or sacrifice beyond her means to make her family happy and contented. No matter the circumstances, she will never fail her children. She will always be there to give moral support, comfort and sympathy, while holding their hands. She is an anchor in the midst of a storm. She is the one who can be relied on. Children know they can place their confidence in her love.

Mothers are seen by her children at her best, full of fun and laughter. They've seen her at her at her worst, with anger and fire in her eyes, tears flowing. Some of those tears are shed for her children when they are out of her sight and protection. She is never content until all her family is tucked safely into bed at night. She breathes a sigh of relief when the last child is asleep.

No one else can be as stubborn as a Mother when she knows her decision is best for her child. She knows where to draw the line at their foolishness, while using the voice of authority. She leans heavily on Dad to drive her point home at times.

Mothers love their husband, their children and grandchildren (babies are her weakness). She loves to sing them a lullaby while rocking them to sleep. She loves to talk with her teenagers, working side by side with her husband. Preparing a well set, full course dinner for family and friends, soft furry animals, shopping, beautiful flowers, pretty clothes that she can dress up in for her family. She loves to dress up her children in their Sunday best, show them off to others. A good friend to tell her problems to, and know her secrets will be held close to their heart.

She does not like door-to-door salesmen, her neighbor's barking dogs, unfriendly, inconsiderate, rude people, or unmannerly, disobedient children. Her sore spot is a bossy mother-in-law.

A mother has the faith and assurance of Apostle Paul, the wisdom of Solomon, the strength and courage of King David. Like Peter, she has the bravery and boldness to stand up against all odds. Teaching her children to be honest, to stand up for things that are good and right. She will let no one hinder their growth or their progress, else she will become a mean fighting machine. She prepares well for her household, she sees they are well-fed, and properly taken care of.

The Proverbs of Solomon says, "She will do you good and not evil all the days of her life. Her price is far above rubies. The heart of her husband does safely trust in her. Her children rise up and call her blessed."

Yet when her world is falling apart around her, the storms of life tossing her in every direction, her children can calm the troubled waters by simply saying, "Mom, I love you."

Fiddle-Faddle

Dad-burn my hide.

A conversation between two neighbor women, I call Sarah and Jane in a bygone era where most folks slaughtered the English language. Being one of the old-timers, I remember and can relate to that lingo (off the wall, so to speak). Surprisingly, a lot of those old sayings and clichés are still around today. How about these little nuggets: Sticks and stones may break my bones, but words will never hurt me; People who live in glass houses shouldn't throw stones; or, he fell down and skint his what'cha ma call it and bruised his somewhat. The scene opens in a humble home on a hot afternoon in Arkansas. In the home of Sarah:

Sarah, as always is busy in the kitchen, when she hears a knock. Wiping her hands on her apron, she rushes to the door. "Well, howdy neighbor. Come on in. Pull up a chair, set a spell. Take a load off your feet. How are you, Jane? Haven't seen you in a coon's age."

Jane: "Howdy, Sarah. I'm just plum tuckered out. My feet are pert neart dragging my tracks out." Wiping the sweat from her face, she says, "Old Man sun is hotter than blue blazes, and I'm as dry as a board."

Sarah: Sarah rushes to get her a fresh dipper of water and hands her a homemade fan. "There's nothing like a good drink of water on a sizzling day like this. Here, drink up."

Jane: "I've sort of got the mully grubs. Thought if I could come over and jaw with you awhile, maybe I could get over these cotton picking blues." Pulling off her bonnet, she laughs and says, "Listen to me going on. No wonder my clothes are getting a mite tight. My John tells me I'm as strong as an ox. Always the kidder. He says when we find the pot of gold at the end of the rainbow, I can carry my weight in gold. I don't see any chance of me carrying any gold right now, our pocket book is flat as a flitter. I shore don't see any dollar signs floating around either. My ol' Daddy tried to tell me when we got hitched there would be days like this. Life ain't always a bowl of cherries, he said. There would be days we would haft to eat sour grapes and live on humble pie. Thank you, Sarah. That good

50

drink shore hit the spot. You've got the best well water here abouts in the whole country."

Sarah: Ain't that the truth. We shore do have a good well. Mr. Oale the water witcher found this sweet water right here in our back door. I've said more times than I can remember, thankee, Lord."

Jane: Wiping sweat and fanning vigorously. "Here I am Sarah, over forty years old, over the hill they say. I don't see this country prospering any ways soon. It's the same old same old, living from hand to mouth. Law me, the president said he has a plan called the New Deal. New Deal my foot. It's more than likely another bitter pill to swallow. What's the world coming to, anyway? Listen to me, here I am talking a blue streak. How are you and the family? By the way, where are the younguns?"

Sarah: Oh, they're around somewhere about the place fiddling around at their own rat killing." She laughed. "But there ain't no flies on my bunch. When they get a whiff of my corn pone and beans, they'll come tearing in here, like a storm, hungry as a ba'r, looking like drowned rats and smelling like deads one to boot. I think Joe snuck out of here with his Sunday overalls on, too. He's gonna catch the devil, when his daddy gets home.

Jane: "Have you heard the latest news? Santa Claus came to Mary and Jim Temples house a couple of days ago and left them a bundle of joy. A little boy. They say he is as cute as a bug's ear, with a head full of black hair and the purtiest blue eyes. Gertie, the mid-wife swears he's a chip off the old block. They haven't put a handle on him yet, meanwhile, they are calling him Jim's Dandy. What's in a name anyways? He will probably get lost in the shuffle later on among those five knot-headed girl children. Daddy Jim is setting tall in the saddle and crowing like a banty rooster perched on a picket fence. He shore is walking in high cotton, strutting like a peacock."

Sarah: "Sadie and Harry over in the Hollow are fighting again, like cats and dogs. I swan, I never heard such goings on. Seems as if she caught him with his hand in the cookie jar, caught him red-handed like a rat in a trap, fooling around some little floozy over in Clay County. He's gone too far this time. He's pulled her chain one time too many. Sadie is mad as an old wet hen and the fur is about to fly. He's got more trouble than he can shake a stick at. If he knows what side his bread is buttered on, he will walk the chalkline. All I can say is, if he was a man of mine, I'd tie him up in a bed sheet and beat the tar out of him. Anyway, they say the little tramp is as ugly as a mud fence. All her powder, paint, and cheap perfume don't improve her looks a bit. If you ask me, Harry's ladder don't quite reach the roof."

Sarah (continued): "Aunt Sophie Brown is sick again—have you seen her lately? She has fell off to almost nothing, skinny as a bean pole. Doesn't eat enough to keep a bird alive. One eyed and snaggled toothed, she looks like she is on her last leg. Wrung out like a dish rag. Pore old soul. It's no wonder—worrying over that no account daughter of hers. She's so lazy she wouldn't move if the house caught on fire. It's been rumored she will inherit a passel of money when her mother passes over. She's just waiting for the undertaker to come get her. Knowing her, she'll run through every thing Aunt Sophia has worked so hard for all these years. Bless her little pea-picking heart. Aunt Sophia wouldn't hurt a fly either. She deserves better than that. If she was my daughter, I'd straighten out the kinks in her back. It gets my dander up every time I think about it."

Jane: "No, I haven't seen or heard anything about her. Speaking of getting old, seems like I'm as old as the hills. I do declare, if I ain't running a race with Father Time. My get up and go has got up and went. My lumbago is acting up. I have a crick in my back (she laughs). I believe I have gun powder in the seat of my drawers. I guess I'm gonna haft to rake up some hard earned money somehow and buy me some of those store bought eye glasses. Money is scarce as hen's teeth around here, but I can't see worth a durn. I do believe these dang youngsters have a bottomless pit. They are about to eat us out of house and home. If they aren't out-growing their clothes, they need a pair of shoes. I think they study on stirring up a can of worms. It gets so wearisome at times I take to my bed. You should see them sing, "Calf Rope," then. They give their chores a lick and a promise. I tell them to lick their calf over. They don't appreciate that little bit of wisdom for some reason. I wouldn't take the price of a new rope for nary one of them though. I love them to pieces."

Sarah: "I know what you mean. I feel the same way about mine. At times they can be a pain in the be-hind, but whatever would we do without them?"

Jane: (laughing at her own joke) "I figured out a way to get them out of my hair for awhile. I says, go climb a tree and skin a cat. Buddy, my youngest took me at my word, and grabbed the cat. You never heard such caterwauling old Tom was doing. I said "Buddy, what are you doing?" He said, "Why ma, I'm trying to skin the cat like you told us to." If that wasn't a sight, him setting up there in that tree like a possum, tormenting that pore thing. That little piece of advice like to back-fired on me. Yet I notice the cat didn't hang around the back door for a few days."

Sarah: (laughing up a storm). "I guess you could call that little morsel a cat's Aunt Jane. Ain't that just like a trifling young'un?"

Jane: (with a twinkle in her eye). "As for old Tom, he was no worse for the wear. Oh, did you hear the latest news? Old man Rufus Hunt and Bob Cates, two of the biggest scoundrels around town, don't you agree? Well, anyway, they both went on a tiff last Saturday, higher than kites. Always spoiling for a fight, pushing and shoving until some brave soul standing in the background said, "Sic 'em Fido." Rufus called Bob chicken livered, then Bob turned around and called Rufus a yellow-bellied skunk. That was the last straw. The fight was on. Smelling of rot gut whiskey, and cussing a blue streak, they oughta been run out of the country on a rail or hanged with a new rope."

Sarah: "Well, if that don't beat a hen a'pecking. They say there is nothing like an old fool. They tell me Bob's heart isn't too good either. That's a good way for him to kick the bucket. It makes a body's stomach turn. All of the kit and caboodle of that family would be better off without the old codgers. I feel sorry for their wives and young'uns, but what's a body to do? If you stick your nose in other folk's family life, you get yourself into a heap of trouble. Oh, those two are running a race with the devil. I'll tell you it's a rotten shame too. We both have good men. They treat us and the young'uns real well, keep a roof over our heads, and grub on our table. They are not out chasing every skirt they can find either. We may be as pore as Job's turkey, but riding the gravy train ain't what it's propped up to be either. Proof is in the pudding, I allus say. Pore old man Jones's no account son has been riding his daddy's gravy train for years, claiming he's under the weather. Under the weather my foot. He looks strong as an ox. If you ask me, he ain't worth a tinker's damn, or the lead to blow him up with."

Jane: "Yeah, I know, but he's able to prowl all over the countryside chasing after every little feisty girl he can find. He's got the ugliest mug I ever saw. I don't see any pretty, decent girl wanting to look at that face every day. (Grinning from ear to ear,) Yeah, he's bound to look like a monkey when he grows old."

Sarah: "You hit the nail on the head when you said that. I thank my lucky stars every day for my man. He shore does make a good bed fellow on a cold winter's night with toasty feet, cuddled up to his best side; we are as snug as a bug in a rug. Dad burned, if I don't love that man. He shore does tickle my fancy! I don't tell too many people this, but he calls me his little Kewpie doll. Imagine that—after all these years."

Jane: "Yeah, I know what you mean. John and me are like two peas in a pod. We stick together like glue. We sort of go together like butter and molasses, smeared on a biscuit. Ah, sweets for the sweet, I say. I don't haft to worry about him pulling any monkey shines on me or flirting around with the devil either. Talking about the devil, we certainly saw him last week lolling around on the streets in town. To make a long story short, the news man on the radio called for rain. Since we were short on grub, we decided to go into town to stock up. So me and the kids and their daddy took off a day to see the sights in town on Saturday. That ole wagon seat got pretty hard before we got there. It was worth the trip though, just to get a cold soda pop. Well anyway, as I said, this character was sitting on the street corner dressed in rags with a pair of gum boots on his feet, dirty as a pig. Long straggly beard and hair. Looked like rats were nesting in it. He was one scary looking dude. So ugly his face would stop an eight day clock, what you could see that is. Like to scared the young'uns to death. Didn't make me feel any too good myself. Of course, the young'uns daddy was off somewhere gabbing with his cronies. I tell you, Sarah, he was plum pitimus. Can't imagine where he came from. You know when we passed by, I heard him mutter under his breath, "Stuck up." Imagine the likes of him calling us stuck up. Oh, well, I allus say, you can't always judge a book by its cover. Just an old down and outer, more than likely. Anyway, we took another route when we got ready to go home. I think he would have spooked the mules."

Sarah: "I'm glad we missed the show, but talk about raining. The newsman was right. Did you ever see such a gully washer Monday evening as we had? The old fogey who lives on the hill, blind as a bat, and crazy as a loon, swore it rained cats and dogs."

Jane: "I'm just thankful we didn't get caught out in it. We would have been caught up the creek without a paddle. With no place to go. In that case I don't think I would have asked John a penny for your thoughts. (Laughing) He would probably have tossed a water-logged pillow at me. I guess there is another side to every thing—you never miss the water till the well runs dry. (Jane looks up at the clock.) Lands sakes, will you look at the time. How the time has flown. By the time I get home, feed the chickens, gather the eggs, milk old Jersey and fix supper for my brood, it will be time to hit the hay. It shore has been good talking to you, Sarah. I feel like a new woman already. Good friends like you are hard to find. (Jane gets up to go.) Ya'll come. I'll cook up a mess of vittles that will stick to your ribs. I'll stir up a pore man's cake to go with it."

Sarah: "Thankee, Jane. We'uns will do that soon and I'll bring along my little tidbit too. (Sarah walks Jane to the door and with a pat on the back says,) Ya'll come."

Jane: (gets in a parting shot) "Seems like I'm allus over here (grinning). If you want me out of your hair for a while, guess you will hafto tell me to go climb a tree and skin a cat. Can you imagine me climbing a tree?"

Sarah: "Fiddle Faddle, Jane. You know you are always welcome. My door is always open to you and yore kin. There has been a lot of water under the bridge since we met. We'uns have drunk from the same well for years. Seems most of our young'uns grew up, and we put our feet under each others tables many times. You and I have cried on each other shoulders since way back when. Why we are just family anyway, and it pleasures me you are feeling better. (Jane walks away.) See you in the funny papers."

With a sigh, Sarah flops down in her favorite chair, fanning herself with her apron. "I declare, that woman just about talks my ears off. I'm as tard as if I'd worked all day in the kitchen. I just wish she would tame her tongue a bit, for it shore does get wearisome how she goes on. Shame on you, Sarah Thompson. Ain't you a little hard on pore old Jane? Bless her heart, she is as good as gold and a good neighbor as well. Oh, well, it will probably come out in the wash. Dad-burn my ornery hide anyway."

(An hour later her family comes in and catches her asleep, while the rafters vibrates with her snores. Waking up, she hears her offspring say, "Wake up, ma. Our bellies is about to meet our backbone, we're as hungry as a ba'r!"

Dearly Beloved

"Today we are gathered together in the sight of God, and in the presence of these witnesses…"

The ceremony had begun. The minister's voice rang out loudly in the stillness of the small room that was bathed in a soft light.

The bride was dressed in a plain simple dress (although it was new). The top consisted of white organdy trimmed in a soft print with a skirt to match, and her feet were clad in a pair of black heels. Looking in the mirror after getting dressed, she didn't have on just an ordinary dress and shoes; she was Cinderella in all her finery, wearing silver slippers on her feet.

She had spent most of the morning getting dressed for her special day. Their wedding would be one of a kind, for it was Heaven sent (or so they thought). With a touch of make-up on her cheeks and lips, with her long black hair curled and cascading down her back, lying softly around her face like a shiny halo sparkled like black gold. Gliding across the floor on magic feet, she knew she looked her best. Her Prince Charming was dressed in a uniform of the United States Army. Standing by her side in a soldier's stance, with his cap placed ever so slightly over one eye, covering most of his close cropped hair, the green in his eyes could not hide the pride and happiness as he looked at his bride. Like Cinderella and her prince, they too, would create their own castle inside her small 10x15 room in the family home. Oh, yes, they made a pretty picture against the background of a sparkling clean room in the minister's home in a country setting.

The minister's voice cut through her thoughts as she heard him say, "Marriage is an institution of divine appointment and an important step in life and should not be entered into lightly, but carefully and soberly."

Her thoughts began to race around in her head like a precocious child, flitting here and there. She wondered if she was prepared to live with this young soldier boy standing by her side—forever. The glamour and prestige of being a soldier's wife would fade once the war was over, when she would be just an ordinary housewife. Could their love stand the test of time and an ocean apart? He was destined, after a two week furlough, to go overseas.

World War II was raging furiously on this their wedding day, April 10, 1944. In a few days, he would be gone away, holding her heart and her thoughts in his hands. Death could be their destiny. But for today, the war was far away where it couldn't touch them, for this day they would savor every moment. Every moment had to be cherished and held close, snatching happiness while they could. For the two weeks they had left, fear would not be their bed partner.

"In this estate, these two people come now to be joined in Holy Matrimony. If any person present can show just cause why they may not be lawfully joined together, let them speak now, or forever hold their peace."

Remembering big sister's words that were spoken with tears in her eyes, at that moment, she was tempted to run back to the safety of her arms, the only mother the bride had ever known. Her sister's last words rolled through her mind in a flash. "Think about what you're doing. Please wait until the war is over, at least you will have plenty of time!" Wait was a cruel word for young lovers. Stealing a glance at her man gave her confidence as she felt his love reaching out to her. All her doubts and her sister's words flew out the door and were forgotten. Think and wait—oh no, they had no intention of doing that for there were mountains to climb, bridges to cross, oceans to span, paradise to discover and explore for at least two weeks. There were dreams to fulfill. No one existed but the two of them. They were on an island of their own.

Waiting was the essence of their future, but not today and the few days they had left. At that moment, she knew she would stand by her man, for she had already pledged him her heart.

"I solemnly require and charge you both as you hope for joy and happiness in this marriage state, if either of you know any just cause why you may not be lawfully joined together in Holy Matrimony you do now confess." After a brief pause, the minister said, "You may now join right hands."

Joining hands they felt was a link to the pledge they were about to make. In her heart, she knew she had made the right choice, the right decision, at the right time, right now.

With the atmosphere cloaked in excitement and with stardust in his eyes, he reached for her left hand and held it all through the ceremony, never realizing his mistake. Not calling his hand was her first commitment to her man. Today there was no war. They were on a merry-go-round spinning, spinning, hoping it would never stop. It was hard to concentrate on the minister's words with her mind in such a turmoil, yet she dimly heard him say, "You may place the ring on her right hand."

She made sure there was no mistake this time for she held out her right hand as he nervously slipped a plain wedding band on her finger. She saw that ring as a diamond solitaire that matched her gown and her silver slippers. But no matter, she would wear that ring forever. It represented a circle not to be broken.

"Joe, will you take this woman to be your wife, will you commit yourself to her happiness and her self-fulfillment as a person and her usefulness in God's kingdom?"

In a quivering voice, he said, "I do." The minister repeated the same words to her and in a voice barely above a whisper, she said, "I do."

"You may kiss the bride."

We needed no prompting to share our first husband and wife kiss. Bells and rockets exploded. Music of our own making followed us as we raced out of the house hand in hand to a brand new life, as those words echoed in our rapidly beating hearts. Hold, touch, taste, drink, savor. Dreams are for today. Tomorrow may be too late.

Getting a letter from a loved one or a good friend is always rewarding. My mind on good news, I thought how nice it would be if one could get an email or a big newsy letter from "Beyond the Grave."

My Dear Beloved:

Fifteen years ago, they told me you had died.
I did not believe those dreadful words for
often the south wind blows me a hardy kiss.
Clasping the wonder in my embrace,

I feel a gentle touch and I know-
It is you.

Watching a graceful bird in flight
I hear a freedom song. He Set Me Free
Its magic lingers in my heart and I
hear a whisper of Love's Old Sweet
Song. You Are My Sunshine and I know-
It is you.

On a bright spring morning the
trees wearing their beautiful green
apparel waves a cheery Good Morning
Dear. I catch an image of a
familiar face and I know-
It is you.

I bask in the radiance of the rising
sun on a summer day, covering me
with its warmth and elegant beauty, even
the rain comes tapping at my window
pane, my door is always open,
for I know-
It is you.

Fantasy and youth often invades
my garden of memories as they
dance among the flowering daisies
and daffodils. Its gardener
is a farmer clad in a checkered shirt,
a favorite pair of blue jeans
and a pair of new working boots
and I know-
It is you.

Time after time I hear the coo of
a morning dove calling its mate.
I respond to the call and answer. "Here I am,"
Searching through the brambles of life, I lose the call—

afraid, and it is then that I cry. Even so, I believed-
It was you.

Although the south wind doth blow
freedom still rings, a spring or
summer day may fall, fantasy and youth may
tiptoe through the flowering garden,
a lonely call may be heard. Yet reality's
child loudly proclaims-
It is you.
Forever yours, Euple

October In Review

I've never seen anything as lovely as a tree...Only God can make a tree...

October in Northeast Arkansas surrounded by a forest of trees flamboyant with color is a beautiful sight to behold.

As October shows its face, the Master Artist digs out his paint and brush as he transforms the trees into brilliant shades of rust, gold, red and yellow. No canvas is ever complete without splashes of green, so the giant cedar escapes His brush.

The hillsides and valleys resemble a huge bon-fire setting the landscape aflame with beauty and magic. Perfection spreads out in a panoramic view as the renowned artist steps back, admiring His art work as He proclaims, "It is good."

The wind takes up the temp of a frolicking beat, as the lazy old sun rolls around in its huge blue orbit, giving light and warmth to the scene as all creation bows its head in reverence. Late blooming flowers strutting their stuff, scrambles across the forest floor while hundreds of butterflies cavort playfully among them and sip sweet nectar from their open blossoms.

Behold, the stage is set for a "Fall Festive." A festival always calls for a feast, and the consummate artist opens up the Heavens to provide manna and sweet nectar for his stately subjects, as a side dish called ambrosia is there to appease the kingly monarchs.

Act 1

Anticipation and excitement begins to build as the curtain goes up on a grand performance. The spot-light focuses on the elegantly dressed trees, both small and great, who begin to clap their limbs with glee, their bright, colorful costumes swirling and flashing in the wind. Sunlight sways with the tempo of the wind. Human spectators taking in the drama, applaud the beautiful art work with pleasure as they shout, "Bravo! Bravo!"

Never was a stage scene ever clothed in such style and beauty. In such a setting, Van Gogh's masterpiece would fade into obscurity in comparison. Flying overhead and through the tree branches is a choir of feathered friends—winging their way further south, thrilling their audience with a melody of poetical compositions.

The cedar trees realizing they are still wearing their old coats are ashamed, so they bow their heads in disgrace. The Master, seeing their shame knew he had made no mistake. Whispering soft and low, he said, "There is no cause to be ashamed, lift up your lofty heads. It's okay to be different. Bright colors do not a Monarch make."

Responding to the voice of authority, they sprang to attention as they join their other counter parts in a toe-tapping caper, titillating the forest floor. Freedom ran rampant as they lost all inhibition of displacement.

Magic and intrigue stalks the forest floor as the giant oak, maple, hickory and walnut rob gallons of condensation from a free flowing creek nearby. A family of coyotes lifts up their voices as they chant a victim's funeral dirge. A lone fox slinks among the trees bent on murder and mayhem, his bushy tail flaring in defiance of all who gets in his way. The law of nature seems to be sleeping on the job as the noisy gray and red squirrels scamper up heavy laden trees, stealing hickory nuts and walnuts out from under unsuspecting eyes as they stash their loot in a hidden retreat high in a hollow tree.

A clamorous red-headed woodpecker from his lofty perch fires off his revolver in quick succession as he devours his prey with relish. A huge owl spying a small animal glides soundlessly to the ground as it pounces on an unsuspecting victim and the curtain falls on the first act.

Act II

The next scene compliments the portrayal of the Garden of Eden-like atmosphere as a dirty brown colored serpent weaves its way through the tree branches and along the forest floor, hissing its hatred at all creation as it glides under a huge boulder. A family of deer showing off their stately bearing, jumps and twists with pleasure for a brief interlude before settling down to a much needed rest. Coyotes and their kindred still their voices and the frisky squirrels munch on nourishing food from their store-house. Wild turkeys boasting loudly of their presence suddenly tuck their heads under their wings standing immobile for they perceive the smell of snow in the air.

Act III

After a brief interlude November begins to blow its trumpet. Its harsh ugly tones blast out October's retreat. Weary, exhausted performers slip off their rumpled ball gowns where it lies at their feet. Pulling up a warm wooly blanket, they fall into a dreamless sleep as the final curtain comes down on a grand finale.

The old watergate

If Walls Could Talk

Since walls can't talk, the mistress of the house who was here from the beginning can be my voice. Since I am a part of history, names, places and time will be listed.

Mr. and Mrs. Joe Riney purchased a 160 acres of woodland to build a house on, for $800.00 in the late 1940's in Randolph County on Washington Road (a dirt road at the time), four miles south of Maynard, Arkansas. They later sold off 80 acres for pasture land, leaving them 80 acres for livestock and cultivation. Milk cows, dairy cows, horses, mules, sheep, goats and pigs roamed around the pastureland that helped feed them. I guess you could say this was an Old McDonald farm, with the old rooster waking the household every morning before daybreak. All this blended into the voice of Mama, Daddy and five children. Ah, Home Sweet Home.

There was often jangling discord among the ensemble until the Maestro brought order and quiet back to the class.

Grief stalked the portal of my walls when members of the family passed away. The mistress's dad (Herman Tutt) in 1967, her companion of forty-seven years (Joe Riney) in 1991, a son-in-law (Frankie Cook) in 1992, a brother-in-law (Carmie Caldwell) in 1992. A sister-in-law (Grace Tutt) in 1997. Brother (Herbert Tutt) in the year 2000. We nurse our grief together she and I for many days. The tears she shed were heart-breaking and sad, whereas mine flowed beneath a wall of wood.

Five children were conceived in the marriage bed. Mickey Joe the first born on November 26, 1946. Fourteen months later on February 18, 1948, Dickey Bren, our second son was born. Our third child, a girl, Rhonda Lynn, was born on July 2, 1949. Six years later on November 16, 1955, Thea Regina came along. At the age of forty-one, Mama had her last child on March 9, 1967, Stephanie Renee. Five healthy children made my old walls rock while my beat-up floors ricocheted with the Jitterbug. If one looked closely you could see my old stockade walls swaying with pleasure.

Quarrels often broke out and angry words were spoken that caused me to sigh with discontent, as I sympathized with them. Although my wooden face never showed any evidence of

65

surprise. After all, they were typical children who one minute were fighting and the next minute, holding hands.

Wedding bells rang out five times as all my children said to their mates, where thou goest, I goest. Mick and Carol Zaboray, Dick and Ruthan Lassen, Rhonda and Ted Byrd, Regina and Frank Cook, who later married Tom Williams after Frank's death. Stephanie and Mark Godwin, who later married Tim Tidwell, where they in turn carved out their own place in time, but unfortunately, didn't stay together. After that my old walls settled down into an entirely different period, with just Mama and Dad.

When a big old black snake found its way into the house years ago, there was fear and chaos. With those slimy coils writhing across my walls, I shivered with fear for my family. Adding to the noise and confusion of a snake in the house was Mama screaming as she did the St. Vitus dance until that creature was captured. At a much later date, another one crawled up the drain pipe into the commode and left its skin wrapped around a tissue box lying nearby. Thank the Lord, no one ever found the snake. But for days Mama was afraid to walk across a dark room. She looked under the bed, terrified she would find it curled up in a dark corner or in a closet. An alarm of overwhelming fear and panic shook Mama's whole body into mush. In her mind, it was a two-headed slimy reptile from the Marshes of the Black Lagoon.

The welcome mat curled around the feet of hundreds of people who passed over our threshold as they soared into my chambers. I smiled with pleasure when my house was clean. If not, my mistress and I were embarrassed.

A gentle breeze skipped through an open window and embraced a sleeping child, lingering like a soft caress. Long tendrils of sunlight streaked across my well-worn floors that warmed and tickled children's feet. I never complained when my wooden face was often smeared with childish artwork. At the unveiling, I wondered why Mama raised such a hullabaloo. Tears my family shed were my weakness, although no one saw, I cried too. Ah, but when laughter and joy was heard, I clapped my hands with gusto and sang a new song along with Mama and her charges. Music and song camped on my doorstep and danced across the floor at the beat of drums and guitars.

My house is a far cry from the small two room cabin the family moved into in 1949. A few years later the Mister built another two rooms onto the back where my family lived until the early 1960's, when they built me. A much bigger version of five rooms and a bath in the 1980's. A glass enclosed back porch was added on and my family enjoyed all the comforts of home at the push of a button and the flick of a switch. TV, microwave oven, refrigerator, washing machine, gas heat, electric cook stove and air-conditioners grace this home today in 2005, making life so much simpler when we had none of those things fifty years ago. Moving day was a day of rejoicing for the lady of the house. Whatever would she do with all this space? It didn't take long to fill up and she proclaims she still doesn't have enough room. In 2003, daughter Stephanie built on to my backside, an addition that included a big bedroom with a walk-in closet, a bathroom, dining room, kitchen and big living room and a pantry. The back porch became a laundry room and a hall between our walls. My outside walls are painted a beautiful honey tan and when the sunlight gleams over my façade, I stand out as a relic of the past, who has sheltered only one family, serving them with love, dignity and pride.

Joe Riney, my owner and Tom Williams, a son-in-law (a master carpenter) made me what I am today. Like the joys of sunlight, a delightful spring rain, the voice of a thousand frog choir that rocked the family inside asleep. I also sighed with relief and bade the family goodnight.

The matriarch of the clan is still weaving the voice of the past as she hears the whisper of her lover, the voice of babies, small children (hers and others) at play, teenagers, wedding bells and grandchildren. My floors have vibrated with the sound of running feet and growing children. Tears were often the bed pillow as one or the other members mourned their fate. All I could do to give comfort was a silent salute to the old adage. "This too shall pass." With each stroke of the pen these old walls stand as a prelude to the little log cabin that once stood on top of a hill, known as the Riney place.

A minister and minister's wife became the parent's way of life in the early fifties, where life was often hectic and nerve wracking. People from all walks of life passed through my door and were welcomed with open arms, where they were consoled and comforted with the words of Jesus Christ, "Come unto me, all ye who are weary and I will give you rest."

December 14, 1991, at the seventy-year-old matriarch's funeral, hundreds of mourners passed by his coffin in a tearful, loving tribute to a man called, "Old Joe." The people who came calling between my walls in those days of mourning, I shared their grief with the wife and children, as my old sturdy walls settled a little lower under the load.

The man called Dad in this household was a day laborer at Sallee's Handle Mill in Pocahontas, where he was a shipping clerk and a painter for over thirty years. On weekends, he took on the task of ministering to others, while Mama sang his songs. *The Old Rugged Cross. How Great Thou Art, Blessed Assurance, Hold to God's Unchanging Hand,* and *How Beautiful Heaven Must Be* and others, would float over the airwaves in harmony with nature. Music and the word echoed over the hills of Arkansas at Johnson's Chapel, Gravesville, The Church of Jesus Christ and at Elmont in Supply. He pastored for many years there. It was situated on the beautiful Current River, where many people were baptized under his ministry. Here she speaks for herself: for I have the rewarding words and ministry to rejoice over today, as I hear the voice of my son, Dick, proclaiming the life and death of Jesus Christ.

My inside walls are covered with knotty pine, sealed with Gem Seal and covered with clear varnish in the living and dining room. The rest of the walls are covered with wallboard and have been painted many colors over the years as my mistress tickles my backside with a pretty shade of blue, yellow and pink paint. Sturdy oak boards and tongue and groove hardwood floors with a sturdy concrete foundation makes up my old house. Sweat, blood and tears have run down my walls, staining my well-worn carpets, but I've held up well. A modern bathroom with lovely hot and cold water was added in the late sixties or early seventies that gladdened the heart of my family.

Meals were sometimes a skimpy affair while at other times the family ate high on the hog. I never told any one Mama and Daddy's secrets they whispered in each other's ears, but I heard and chuckled along with them. They never knew I was listening, yet they knew I would never tell. When my mistress joins the mister, I hope I am grateful for all our years together. I believe I have served them well. In the distance of time, I hear the sweet refrain, "Swing Low Sweet Chariot, coming for to carry me home."

This Old House

This old house once knew my children
This old house once knew my wife
This old house was home and shelter as we fought the storms
    of life
This old house once rang with laughter
This old house heard many shouts
Now she trembles in the darkness when the lightnin' walks
    about

Ain't gonna need this house no longer
Ain't gonna need this house no more
Ain't got time to fix the shingles
Ain't got time to fix the floor
Ain't got time to oil the hinges
Nor to mend the window pane
Ain't gonna need this house no longer
I'm getting ready to meet the saints

This old house is getting shaky
This old house is getting old
This old house lets in the rain and
This old house lets in the cold
On my knees I'm getting chilly
But I feel no fear or pain
'Cause I see an angel peeking through
A broken window pane

Now my old hound dog lies asleeping

He don't know I'm gonna leave
Else he'd wake up by the fireplace
And he'd sit there, howl and grieve
But my hunting days are over
I ain't gonna hunt the 'coon no more
Gabriel done brought in chariot
When the wind blew down the door.

Composed and written by Stuart Hamblen
The Gaither Vocal Band

Images

I woke up one morning before daybreak.
I could not sleep for goodness sake.
Images one by one flashed through my mind

Here and there and everywhere some
were even lagging far behind
Images both small and great,
iridescent and fragile as the
translucent wings of a butterfly.

There I was, a seventy-year-old grandmother about to cry.
I saw a pretty young girl wooed
by a handsome soldier boy,
Dressed in khaki brown who turned
her world upside down.

I caught and held on to a vision
of a wedded pair
She was a picture of loveliness
with flowing black hair.
He was all spit and polish in his
military attire.

Images of age and time, then
I heard The Swan Song
tip-tapping inside my front door
Flinging Heavens portals wide,
I saw my soldier boy dining among
the angels
Residing on the Hallelujah side.

My Dream

A group of people and I were gathered in the concert house when a giant of a man came into our midst. He was crazy, and had the features of a monster; mean and vicious, throwing things and breathing down everyone's neck with a killer heart.

Everyone was scared to death, some considered calling the police (for some reason, we didn't). Everyone was trembling with fear. There were two men in the group who were watching him and seemed to think he could be helped. In the next scene everyone but me and the two men had disappeared.

A man with an orange outfit was in the other room, as I peeked into a small window. I heard the man in orange say, "Turn this man loose." Apparently, he had been restrained at the time.

The man came into the room where the two men and I were alone at this time. Here the most beautiful man entered the room, such a gentle look in his clear eyes and a glow about him. The demented creature that first came into our presence looked like an angel. He opened wide his arms with love radiating from every part of his body and gathered me in his big sweep of an embrace. He held me close to his warm heart. The last scene, I went to see him later in his home where he lived with his mother and dad. He was still a beautiful man who met me with love and another hug. His mother asked me why and how I landed in Arkansas and I said, "This has always been my home and I love it here.

The odd thing about the whole dream was, his name was Joe. My deceased husband's name.

Boys, a Horse and a Hatful of Horse Biscuits

This is a true tale of our two young teenage boys, Mick and Dick. We always had two or three horses on the farm. The boy's rode the back trails of the land or the countryside, often with a group of neighbor boys. They showed off their skills as a cowpoke, riding the range. Ah yes, according to them, they were real cowboys wearing a cowboy hat, a checkered shirt, Levis, and cowboy boots.

Mick had an old scruffy hat he wore practically all day and night. It was shaped just right to fit his head snugly and he wore it with pride. Dick, on the other hand, had rather feel the breeze blowing through his hair.

For some reason, they were riding alone on the back of old Topsy, Mick in the driver's seat. Topsy was a gentle black mare that never lost her cool until things went a little crazy, like the day the boys were riding down a country road near our house. The gravel road began to get a little too much for Topsy's tender feet and she made a dash for the side of the road while Mick tried to pull her back on the road with no success. Fighting the reins, she ran smack dab into a tree so hard it knocked Mick out and he fell under Topsy's belly, between all four feet. By this time, she was so agitated she went into a nervous frenzy, prancing up and down in one spot right over his prostrate body. Luckily, she never stepped on him.

Dick, however, saw what was about to happen, so he jumped to safety. Being in front, Mick got the full force of the impact. Stunned, he lay where he fell, unaware of being in jeopardy. Dick thought his big brother was faking it. Yet the thought did enter his mind, "Why doesn't he get up, the stupid nut?" Still he made no effort to pull him out of harm's way.

Coming to in a few minutes, Mick, seeing his dangerous situation, scrambled to safety. Talk about a tongue lashing, Dick got it. The air was full of hell and damnation, cussing a blue streak was a man's privilege (when Mama and Daddy weren't around, that is).

When he ran out of foul words, he realized he didn't have his hat on. He spied it several feet away, lying upside down on its crown. He retrieved it, slapped it on his head and realized it was full of horse biscuits. It had fell off, landing directly behind Topsy's hind legs. She had discharged her morning meal in one big scoop in his prized hat.

If Dick thought the air was blue before, it was black when he turned his anger on Topsy. Stomping around and cussing some more, the crowning touch came, when he dumped that steaming, smelly dung out of his hat. Turning around, his face showing his contempt for her, he thumbed his nose at her as he jammed his beloved hat back on his head. Hats off to two very cool cowboys and a salute to Dick who hardly ever wore at hat at all.

A hat was too big a bother anyway. There were two rather shamed-faced, subdued teenage boys when they arrived back at the house a few minutes later. That was a subject Mick didn't care to discuss for the time being and Dick was sworn to secrecy.

Today, forty years later, when the tale of "The Horse Biscuits," comes up, the family agrees they were indeed two rooting, tooting, shooting cowpoke's, carrying with them the scent of sweating horse flesh, and the smell of animal dung on their boots, or in this case, Mick's hat.

Since boys like a little diversion now and then, he figured a little horse tonic was good for his black, curly hair that all the girls went crazy over.

Mick, Dick and pet pigeon, Pleonis riding Topsy

Bottles

I have six bottle men setting on my windowsill. Day after day, it seems as if they have their eyes on me, a little smug perhaps, as they see me in all sorts of dress and they've seen a lot of tears I have shed. I'm sure they have silently laughed at some of my shenanigans. Sitting on my windowsill, they seem to be out of their proper setting, all except the country gentleman.

There is Captain Hook with his first mate. A big game hunter, a Scottish bagpipe player and a cassock (or priest). The only one of them that has anything in common with each other is Captain Hook and his mate. They out number the rest of them with their deadly looking guns and swords, although the big game hunter could give them a run for their money with a wicked looking rifle at his side.

He is dressed in a somber brown suit with a darker brown shirt underneath. He wears a red string tie and a brown helmet type hat on his head. His feet are encased in brown boots to match his suit and hat. He has a handlebar mustache with one blue eye and a spy glass covering the other eye. He's holding a grey beady, black-eyed mouse by the tail. Perhaps he has heard the tale of a mouse scaring an elephant. Maybe it would scare an elephant across his vision.

From the Highlands of Scotland, the bagpiper is setting on a stump with a red bagpipe clutched tightly in his arms. He has on a tan vest and tie, and a saucy red cap. His coat and kilts are red; red knee high socks down to his red buckled shoes. Perhaps he is about to play a Scottish rendition of "Roaming in the Gloaming." Looking at his smile, I wonder how many young women he has beguiled with his music and song. Who knows, perhaps he is tuning up to serenade his "Lady Love."

Captain Hook is dressed in a blue captain's coat with blue pantaloons to match, flowing over a pair of black, run down boots. The logo "Skull and Crossbones" are stamped on his blue hat. He has a black patch covering one eye, with a wicked gleam in the other one. His hook hand is helping his other hand hold a vicious looking gun with his finger on the trigger.

The other cut throat, his first mate, is standing nearby. He can't be trusted, for Captain Hook is holding a Treasure Chest between his legs. Woe to the man who tries to steal what's inside. To protect his bounty, he wears a sharp sword at his side. His voice echoes across the water. "Well, Blimy, blow the man down," or "Dead man overboard."

I can see why he doesn't trust his first mate for he is a dangerous looking old sea dog with flashing black eyes and a sullen, turned down mouth. He is sporting a mean looking mustache. Wearing a wine, green and yellow stripped short-sleeve shirt, showing off his muscles, arms covered with tattoos, he has on a pair of yellow pantaloons, slit and tattered, just above his black buckled shoes. He has a wide wine colored cummerbund tied in a bow hanging down his backside that sports a brace of deadly guns. Not only that, he is holding a cutlass across his belly, one hand resting on the blade, honed to a fine edge. Stamped in black across the blade is one word, "Whiskey." To protect his head from the sun, he wears a yellow kerchief tied in a bow over one ear.

The toughest male would quake in terror at this fearsome old Pirate. His greatest delight is when he sights a fine-looking ship to plunder as he proudly proclaims, "Ship ahoy, Captain!"

The country gentleman is my favorite by far, as his big fat belly seems to be rumbling with laughter. His grey mustache and chin beard is covering a gentle smile and his blue eyes are sparkling with mischief. A gray hat is all but covering his gray hair. He has on a red vest with a gold watch chain across his rotund belly. A tan thigh length coat graces his upper body while black pants and gleaming brown shoes covers his lower body. He wears a blue string tie and a red boutonniere in his coat lapel. A Country Gentleman always smokes and he holds a glowing cigar between his left hand fingers. A gentleman always tips his hat to a lady, and I could almost swear he saluted me on a fine Sunday morning by doffing his hat as he said, "Good morning, Mrs. Riney!"

The cassock is residing over the entire group. A wise and learned clergy man who travels around the countryside doing good deeds as he proclaims, "The Good News is Jesus Christ." He has long brown hair and a brown beard that covers most of his face. He's wearing a black bowl-like hat, and a long red flowing robe tied at the waist with a rope-like tassel in the likeness of small green leaves. His blue eyes seem to pierce into the innermost part of men's souls, while giving comfort and hope to all he comes in contact with. In my hour of grief at my husband's death, I distinctly heard him say, "It's all right, Miss Euple. This too will pass."

This is the story of the six bottles that were once filled with liquor. (Although they were empty when I received them as a gift.) The first mate drools with envy as he remembers all these bottles were once full of his favorite drink. From time to time, me thinks, I hear him say, "Ho-ho-ho and a bottle of rum."

The Streaker

Remember the fad of the streaker in the early 1980's? Some brave soul would strip down buck naked and run down the street, across a parking lot or through a shopping mall in their birthday suit. Ray Steven's record, *The Streak*, hit the music world full blast and became an instant hit. "Don't look Ethel," was on everyone's lips all across America.

The Streaker of the 1980's had nothing on one little girl, namely me. For I was the first contender in 1932 to do the streak. My streaking happened on a Saturday afternoon. That's when my big sister washed my hair. For me that was a tragedy. I just knew she was going to drown me as she poured that final rinse water over my head. Bent over a washbasin, with my head practically between my legs, produced sheer panic and fear.

She would strip me naked, for if she didn't, anything I had on would be sopping wet in a few minutes as I always put on quite a show, doing the St. Vitus Dance. With a well-known face soap, Palmolive, running down my face and in my eyes, stinging and burning, I became a screaming, spitting, wild thing. I would have bit her or kicked her if I thought I could have gotten away with it.

The process went on and on, seemingly forever. My sister was never satisfied until my hair was squeaky clean. Then those tangled page-boy tresses were combed out (not brushed) to a shining halo around my head and face. The pain from the combing was almost as bad as the head washing. Stealing a glance in the mirror at my pretty hair, my fear suddenly vanished, until the next Saturday afternoon. Then it began all over again.

Then there was the fateful day things got out of hand. Scared to death, soapy water flying all over the small table, floor, my sister and me, with snot and tears intermingling, I kicked and screamed, eluding my sister's grasp and tore out the back door.

Around and around the house I ran in all my unclad splendor. In plain view of anyone who may have passed by on the road a few feet from our front door, wet hair and soapy suds flying behind me. At that moment, I didn't care if the whole world saw me; I was bent on getting away from my enemy.

79

Going in the opposite direction, Sis caught me as I rounded a corner of the house. I kicked and screamed all the way back inside, feeling as though she was leading me to a firing squad. Inside, she sat me down, locked the door that was too high for me to reach and sternly put me back in front of that hated tub.

Frightened as I was, I had visions of people passing by my coffin, shaking their heads and saying, "Poor little thing, what a pity her sister drowned her while washing her hair." If my race for life had hit the news, I could see the headlines: Miss Tutt who undoubtedly has a killer instinct, finally did her little sister in this week by drowning her while washing her hair at their country home, near a small town of Caruthersville, Missouri. I was probably the fastest streaker ever born.

Streakers of the 1980's were far too late to hold the record of being the first streaker. That title actually belongs to a small mini-sized contestant, who was deprived of her hour of fame and fortune. Who wanted fame and fortune anyway when staring into the face of death?

The old cliché, "What goes around, comes around," caught up with me some thirty years later through the same frightening experience with my youngest daughter. Even with no tears shampoo, she was terrified. Although the two of us never went through The Streak, she did the Bunny Hop all over the bathroom floor.

I guess my little escapade in 1932 could be summed up with three little words:

"DON'T LOOK ETHEL!"

I Never Hear My Mother Sing

Regina Williams

I believe my mother was meant to sing in large cathedrals and opera houses. She was born with music in her heart and as a child; I slept to the sound of her voice singing sweet lullabies. The circumstances in her life at the time reflected her choice of melodies. During her courtship and subsequent marriage to the man of her dreams, she sang *You Are My Sunshine*. When he shipped overseas, loneliness and fear tinged the radiance of her voice when she sang, *No Letter Today*.

My father's safe return filled her with happiness and the words to joyful songs spilled out of her mouth. My parents were young, the world was reborn after the war and there were many songs to sing.

The arrival of five children gave her another reason to sing, as if she needed one, and she entertained us with *Rock a Bye Baby* and *Would You Like To Swing On a Star?* and I always giggled when her voice lowered into mock horror when she got to the part that said, "or would you'd rather be a mule?" And when she crooned, *Twinkle, Twinkle Little Star*, I knew I was her diamond shining brightly in her life. I snuggled down, her work-worn but caring hand gently rubbing my head, and went to sleep with her sweet, gentle voice carrying me into that never-never land where her songs still linger.

Singing was as much a part of my mother as breathing—she needed both to survive. Her soprano voice echoed across the hills and wafted gently through the valleys of our farm on any given day. The strains of a favorite ballad carried on gentle winds let me know I was safe, that everything was perfect in my little world.

Her choice of songs reflected her mood. A bright, cheerful day when soft summer breezes caressed the skin and she was happy, *I'll Fly Away* or a popular song she liked rollicked in the air.

On sad days, when things seemed insurmountable and burdens lay heavy on her heart, *In The Garden* or a sad song of

81

lost loves and desperation floated quietly over the green fields and I, in turn, felt the sorrow in the words and in her voice.

On Sunday mornings, my mother's voice could be heard above the others as she sang of God's love and forgiveness. Her joy bubbled over into her hands and feet that clapped and tapped their way through song after song. No one ever doubted her love for the Creator and his wondrous blessings when she sang.

Glorious spring days found her outside, reaching for God's ears. The house was too small to contain her voice and *How Great Thou Art* would be directed toward the heavens with love and thankfulness for all He'd given her.

When I grew up and married, and living next door, many times as I walked outside, I could hear her voice resounding in the air and I'd smile because that sound, that beautiful, melodious voice still had the power to make me feel safe.

Grandchildren, then later great-grandchildren gave her new generations to sing lullabies to and remember silly little ditties that left them giggling at her antics as she often acted out the songs. *This Little Boy (or Girl) of Mine* was the favorite that encased those children in a blanket of tenderness and warmth as she gently rocked them to sleep.

It didn't matter whether she was planting beautiful flowers or slugging her way through the most menial of chores, my mother's voice lifted on the breeze and songs hovered over the farm in joyous abandon or in drifts of sorrow.

My mother sang. It defined her.

Thirty-six years of my life was lived listening as she sang old songs she remembered from her childhood and teenage years. Gospel songs and popular new tunes built up inside her until they burst forth like a butterfly shedding its cocoon and it spilled out of her no matter where she might be.

Then, one day, her voice was stilled.

My father, the man of her dreams, her handsome soldier boy passed away. The man who always would be, "her sunshine," had left her alone and afraid.

The silence that wrapped the farm where my father walked the fields and strolled through the forest were so palpable it was almost a living thing. I no longer felt safe. Somehow the earth had tilted on its axis and the songs had fallen into a deep, dark abyss and neither my mother nor I knew if it would shift back, bringing happy little melodies with it.

Ever so slowly, it did. The day I stepped outside my home and heard the oh, so familiar strains of *How Great Thou Art*, brought a sense of happiness washing over me and for the first time, in a long time, peace settled in my heart again.

My mother is eighty now. And except for a few health problems, she's doing quite well. She's given up driving and many other things she loved to do that kept her young and happy for so many years. A walker steadies her steps and she doesn't get outside except to and from the car.

I desperately miss hearing her voice carried on the wind to surround me with her love and gentle nature. And while the songs may still reside in her heart and soul, these days, I never hear my mother sing.

Regina

My Grandmother

Jamie (Cook) Johnson

This story has no end, that is to say, it will carry on past mere words as a wonderful life, a life that will be remembered by many. I first met you on September 7, 1979, and I first remember you as the woman who "rocked" me to sleep in one of your straight back chairs. The legs thumped back and forth and your beautiful voice sang me off to dream land without a care in the world.

You had five children, all of whom I love dearly, but I was your sixth child, for you raised me as one of your own. I respect you and try my best to make you proud of me and the woman I turned out to be under a flurry of family influence. I hope I have made everyone proud in one way or another. You once said that you were very proud to be a part of this family. I can tell you that none of us would be the people we are today if it hadn't been for you and Grandpa. You both were role models for us all, and it pains me to think that my children will never know his kind voice or gentle nature.

You, on the other hand, are starting to give them what you gave me so many years ago. Someone they can have fun with, a best friend only a Grandmother can be. All of my family is important to me, and that sense of togetherness you also helped instill. My life has taken many rocky roads and will take more still, but your strength I can only hope to gain as I age. You proved to me that adversity is only misery if you allow it to pull you down into its pit where you can wallow until it drives you mad. You choose to ignore the misery and instead, pull up out of the situation, back on top. I told you that you would come home stronger and feeling more like your old self. I believed it deep in my heart that you would come home, back to your house and beat the odds. You always have in the past and I saw no other option. You have been the glue that has held this family together for years.

Yes, we have our problems, and yes, we are all stubborn. But it is because we are all so much alike, the family sticks together when things go bad. If someone caused a problem for one of us, then they had us all to deal with. It has shown me love like no other family I have seen. I have so many wonderful memories of each of my family members that I will never lose. Since this is a story not only for you, as my Grandmother, but a testament to the family, I will share some of my greatest memories of all of them.

My mother would sing to me before bed at night, my favorite song, *I'm So Lonesome I Could Cry.* I still remember her voice as she sang, and looking into her face as my eyes closed.

My Uncle Dick teaching me what fossils were and agates along with many other rocks found around here. Aunt Ruth for teaching me how to cook, paint and add at her dining room table. Aunt Stephanie for coloring with me and teaching me how to stay inside the lines, and playing with me when no one else had the time. Aunt Rhonda for spending time with just me when we went to visit. Uncle Mick shared his stories, amazing me and holding my attention. (Which everyone knows how hard that was!)

And my Father, taking time to walk in the woods with me, teaching me all the different tracks and signs of the forest. My grandpa for teaching me the ways of a cattle farmer and farm hand, the difference between a normal cow and a Hereford. Nancy, Brenna, Anthony, Dan and I all going for walks in the woods on warm summer days. Bryan for being funny and telling us kids a joke. Uncle Ted, I was always so scared to talk to you, you were so smart. I felt as if I would embarrass myself if I opened my mouth, but now, you are one of the most interesting people I know.

All these people have given me such wonderful memories and now it is time to share some memories of you. Sitting in your old green swing and picking shapes out of the lazy clouds drifting by. Walking in the woods pretending we were on an adventure. Lying on the limestone rocks at your "secret place," as we threw rocks into the creek for Sabana to chase. Making some sort of art in your house, or learning to cook. We watched "Mutual of Omaha's Wild Kingdom," and ate watermelon in the yard. Taking me to church and letting me sing in front of people there, giving me the courage later on to join band in high school, and to be in several of the plays there.

My love of animals and nature I got from you. I know all of our farm, plus many of the surrounding areas through our walks. I also know most of the people in this area because of you and grandpa. It's amazing all the things I see other kids miss out on today that I got to witness everyday as a child. There was no 'bored" in my vocabulary. I always found something to do. Normally, it didn't involve mischief, but I had my moments like any kid. I look back and wish I would've had more time with Dad and grandpa, but the memories of my childhood are good enough. All the memories I have of them seem to stick in my mind and I am transported back to that time in my childhood where everything was simple. But you saw me through this far, and I will always know that no matter what, I can go to you, or anyone in my family for support and guidance. All my life I have wanted to do for others, and I do, whenever I get the chance, but this need may lead me into a career that has promise. I owe it all to you and my loving family. We all have grown under your watchful eye, and have become great things. We have in our family many accomplished people and one day I hope to reach a job title that is greater than any other; I hope one day to be a Grandmother!

Euple and Jamie Johnson Oct. 2006

Grandma's Eyes

Jamie (Cook) Johnson

In my grandma's eyes
I see wisdom
Many years past mine.
In my grandma's life
I see courage
She is so much braver than I.
In my grandma's hand
I see work
So much harder than I ever will.
In my grandma's laugh
I hear so many good times,
The ones we shared in laughter.
In my grandma's soul
I see love.
I know some belongs to me.
In my grandma's face
I see…
Now an old woman…
But one of the best friends
I've ever had.
I love you maw-maw.

Ferdinand the Bull

He was given to me on my twenty-first birthday on December 11, 1946, compliments of my husband. World War II had been over since May 1945 and we were living in our first home down on the farm in a little log cabin along a country road. To help celebrate my birthday, we had a two week old baby boy. Life was good and we were content. Our little two room cabin sparkled with sunshine and happiness as we watched over our baby with pride and devotion, seeing a miraculous change in him every passing day.

My birthday was complete when my man brought out that gorgeous bull. It was love at first sight. No ordinary name for him. I knew right off he was no run-of-the-mill animal. Somewhere down the pages of history, Ferdinand came to mind, thus my bovine friend became "Ferdinand the Bull."

Stroking his head and back, I could tell he was from a special breed, although he came with no pedigree. His coat was a golden tan, resembling a big gob of creamy butter. The markings on his body were very strange. Around his neck he sported a white collar complete with two small red flowers where it came together under his chin, reminding me of two shiny buttons. Over each shoulder was a small red strap, ending midway between his back and his big, fat belly. At the end of each strap in front were two more quarter sized red spots. I made a joke about it and said, "Why Ferdinand, you look like you are wearing suspenders, complete with buttons and a collar, no less." He had a tuff of kinky hair sprouting between his two big horns. I knew by the expression on his face, he wouldn't ever hurt me with those horns. I couldn't keep from smiling as I took in his gentle demeanor and his dreamy eyes. Sizing me up, he stared at me with those big brown eyes as if to say, "You and I will be good friends," all the while flashing me a come hither look. He had a big fat tummy that seemed to rumble with laughter as I tickled his underside.

He lounged around our farm for years, while our family grew. Another boy and three daughters joined our first born, making a total of five children that filled our house to overflowing. A fast growing family is hard to fill up at mealtime

– although Ferdinand seem to have the biggest empty spot to fill. He kept me busy filling his empty pot belly. His favorite food was candy, doughnuts, nuts and cookies, along with a juicy apple now and then.

I remember at one time he took a craving for some grease stained recipes I had collected over the years. I thought that very strange food. But then I remembered reading somewhere that certain papers have salt in them. Perhaps he wasn't getting enough salt in his diet.

With the chores of motherhood, cook and dish washer, I often ignored Ferdinand, but he never seemed to mind. He always welcomed me with the same happy face. He never cared much for a bath, but every so often, I would don a cleaning pad to clean his grimy body. Yet I was always careful not to get soap in his eyes.

The children were never allowed to look after Ferdinand, for they knew he was Mama's pet. Besides they had more exciting things to do, such as playing ball or riding horses. However, they were always stealing his food right out from under his nose when Mama wasn't looking. He endured their thievery and their little grubby hands pulling his ears and kid-handling him, time after time, with patience and endurance. Secretly, I think he enjoyed it all, for out of the corner of my eye, I could swear I saw him stick out his big red tongue and lick those grubby little hands and face, for I often heard a giggle as they sped away from the scene of the crime.

Age has left its mark on Ferdinand. Old as he is, he doesn't care much for sweets anymore. He simply refuses to let me look at his teeth. He bares the scars of an old wound that often trouble me. He got that from a fall when the children were jostling him around. I patched him up the best I could. In gratitude, he gave me that lovely look. Ah, yes, I believe Ferdinand is about ready to be put out to pasture. He has earned his retirement.

As for me, well, I'm not what I used to be sixty years ago either. I'm known as a senior citizen today.

Of all the pets that have come and gone over the years, Ferdinand has been my favorite. We have secrets we will never tell, of bold glances and sweet nothings between my spouse and

I. Stolen kisses no one else saw—only Ferdinand, who looked on, and smiled with pleasure.

He always seemed to gauge my every mood, and sympathized with me when I was sad or angry. If he could have responded in kind, perhaps he would have said, "Cheer up, my friend. Life isn't so bad. Many times I've heard you say, this too shall pass. Let a smile be your umbrella on a rainy, rainy day."

Yes, Ferdinand and I have beautiful memories of good times, loving and sharing with friends and family. Yet we were sad when the children grew up and left our home. There were no more stolen goodies to share. That is, until the grandchildren became sneaky little robbers as well. We were all grief-stricken when my soul mate and the children's father met his untimely death by heart failure. Forty-seven years together was not enough. Could that have been a tear I believe I saw on Ferdinand's cheek?

Yes, Ferdinand has become a legend that dates back to 1946 that delighted a young wife and mother, sitting the pace of six decades together.

For you see, Ferdinand is my favorite cookie jar!

Peace

As a wife, mother and grandmother, I began a long search for peace and contentment. So leaving my humble abode, I sat out on my quest. I went to the mighty Mississippi River. I sat down on its sandy beach and contemplated peace. Surely, I would find peace here as I surveyed its magnificent sweep of water as I listened to the warbling birds along the peaceful tree-lined shore. Then I knew its destruction in days of yore, when it flooded homes and farm lands. No, peace wasn't here.

Then I went to the forest, where it was tranquil and quiet as the giant trees made a canopy of safety and security overhead. Then from out of a darkening sky, thunder boomed and lightning flashed among the trees and along the ground as the rain descended. I knew there was no safety or security in the forest. Seeking shelter, I raced away from the storm.

Then I went to the city of a thousand lights. Surely I would find it among the huge buildings towering high in the sky. Where all the Philosophers and educated flocked to teach of wisdom and knowledge. They surely had the answer to my quest. Then I saw the hungry children seeking food and the homeless lying on the streets without a pillow to soften their resting place. I cried when I saw the masses of hopelessness wandering here and there with no place to call their own. Peace was not in the city of thousands of lives. Broken dreams walked the street day and night, often fading into a nightmare.

Then I went to the mountains, thousands of miles above sea-level, where their lofty heights embraced the clouds soaring across the heavens, quickly fading into infinity. Those mountains were the closest thing to Heaven I could find. Yes, I was sure I would find peace in such a superb setting with pure white, pristine beauty covering many of their peaks. Thinking on the mystery of their greatness and wondering how long they had stood the test of time, I was reminded of mud and snow slides that had destroyed thousands of homes and lives over the years. Then I knew I couldn't find what I was searching for in the mountains.

My travels took me to the seashore, where I heard its powerful roar and viewed its majesty that set my heart to soaring

on the wings of the wind—as it toned a lyric of
"Peace Be Still." Walking along its sandy beaches, picking up
mementoes to treasure, I was comforted for awhile. Then I heard
of a ship at sea swallowed up in its depths with adults and
children aboard. I realized the ocean had no sympathy for death
and carnage. Death was buried beneath its powerful undertow.

Early one morning, my sojourn led me to a secluded spot in
the desert where no living inhabitation lived, except small
animals, snakes, wild plants, and waterless shrubbery. It sang of
an endless vastness of uncluttered space and I drank of its
tranquility. I just knew this was it as I surveyed its marvelous
sand dunes that went on and on that seemed to reach the sky.
Then the hot beaming sun came up and the heat began to
penetrate the very depth of its existence, to a cauldron of
sweltering, burning abyss of fire and brimstone. Suffering from
its cruelty, I was barely able to struggle back to civilization and
cooler temperatures.

I went away disappointed, knowing there was no peace even
in the desert, where anxiety and confusion did not exist. Weary
with my search for what I thought was unattainable. By this time
it was time to go back to the home I'd forgotten about in my
quest for peace. I wondered why I had ever left the comforts of
home. Walking across my threshold, I was greeted warmly and
lovingly by the open arms and smiling faces of my family.

"Ah, peace, that defies all understanding was in the heart of
my own little castle among my own precious kindred. What was
always under my nose had blinded my vision of peace and
safety. "Amazing Grace, how sweet the sound…."

Roses

Three red roses plucked fresh from the vine
The hands that plucked them belong
 to a young man in my life
For he is a son of mine.

In those three roses, a message was read
Mother and son both shared
Word's were not necessary as he
 placed them in my hand.

Walking up the hill to my house
Perhaps a quarter of a mile
out of breath a bit as he entered my domain,
He gave me a hug and a cheery smile.

Handing me his little token with
 a flourish of pride
For you, Mama, put them in a pretty vase
place them near your bedside.

Memories of a little boy came to my mind
as he handed that same mother
a wild bouquet
of spring flowers like Dutchman's britches

Memories are fine but so is today
As in my arms his roses lay.

Communicating with my children is quite rewarding.
Joy no one else can give:
Nothing on earth could ever compete
But roses for Mama—

What a lovely treat!

(Dedicated to my son, Dick)

My Place in the Sun

My favorite place was a little secluded spot deep in the heart of the woods, on a huge boulder jutting out from the bank of a free flowing creek. The singing of the creek running underneath my rocky stage was the music I sang along with. My audience was the birds and wild animals. Out in the distance a squirrel is chattering its music along with me. I hear a woodpecker tooting his horn. His song is silent for a few minutes as he ferrets out a juicy bug from the side of an old rotten tree, while he dines on a delicacy fit for a bird. A big green frog perched nearby, chirps out his rendition of "Froggy Went A'Courting".

There is only the sky overhead as it looks down on my outdoor theater. I see a splattering of blue through the lofty branches of the trees. Sun and shade dapples the rock where I sat, warming the cockles of my heart. I perform well here, for there is no stage-fright, my peers do not complain, nor boo me. Like Cinderella I am a princess for one hour of the day when the performance is over and it's time to go home, I take up the duties of wife and mother. (Let it never be said that my family scorned my singing ability.) Mother's voice was music to the children's ears.

As I lounge on my queenly throne, there is a huge tree just in front of me with a grapevine intertwined in its branches. Becoming a child again, I wonder if I could swing across the creek bed. Yet, I didn't fit the image of Jane in *Tarzan of the Apes*. I soon forgot that idea right away, as I stretched out my tired feet. Yet the child in me kicked off my shoes and dangled them in the cooling depth of the creek, while perched high on my rocky dais.

At times I even waddled across its gravel bed on bare feet. Images of a small child came to mind, for I loved the cooling depth of the woods as I tiptoed across another creek even then. So I guess it was destiny I discovered my little conclave in the wood. No other title is appropriate for swinging over the grand entrance at my Place in the Sun. The backwoods of Arkansas is lovely in the spring with wild flowers and a musical breeze blowing through the lofty trees, acres of trees at the back and an open meadow at the front door. I often sought out its cool turf, lying flat on my back as I dreamed and observed the boiling clouds. I've been known to nap there.

May the music of the meadow with its song of silver streams bring sunshine to the path you walk and magic to your dreams. These words were on a birthday card one of my daughter's gave me, it seemed to fit my "Hideaway in the Sun."

If one doesn't know where this magic spot is, it would miss the eye completely. I stumbled across it years ago by accident while following the creek. Enveloped in its embrace, silence surrounds me and the cares of the world fade away as my thoughts soar into the heavens, for I feel as one with "the God of all living things."

I hear the voice of a friend echoing over the hills of Arkansas in my own private little Garden of Eden, as I hold its unspoiled beauty in my grasp. Never once did the old serpent disturb my rendezvous.

My inner being soars away on wings of peace in my small kingdom, the moss covered rock being my throne. The joy I feel in my heart rises upward, as a lone coyote raises his voice in a mating call and the squirrels chatter happily. Busy traffic is no problem and there isn't a house in sight to mar its beauty.

As all the children left the nest, and my husband passed away, "My Place in the Sun," was my refuge in times of need as I cried and talked to the Master on High. My tears were soon dissolved in a song of a mockingbird, then I whistled along with him, a song of victory.

The flowers growing along my creek bank cannot compare to the flower in heaven's garden. My husband is busy checking out that garden and one day in the future, he will show me the way.

Memories, dreams and sweet music of a lost love, still linger in my heart. As an eighty-year-old grandmother many times over, that is enough for now.

Snake Tales

Snakes have always been my worse enemy. Little snakes, big snakes, and any in between. Seeing one terrifies me into a hysterical frenzy. My feet and legs have no mind of their own as they do the St. Vitus dance. I have no control over my trembling hands and arms, my voice is several octaves higher as I screech out an alarm in a voice petrified with fear.

In the summer of 1948, Joe and I had two small boys, actually babies as they were four and eighteen months. We lived in a small three room house with a front and back porch attached. It was at the end of a tree lined road.

We were sort of isolated from society on a small run-down farm, but we were content in our little conclave in the woods. We had a pair of mules named Bill and Tobe, a milk cow, a flock of chickens and a fattening pig or two, vegetables eaten out of the garden and wood for winter's use. Joe, always a farmer, farmed a small plot of land.

We also had a hand dug storm cellar catty corner from the front gate. Storm cellars were very common at that time. Most of them were dug out of the dirt and shored up with logs. Very few were concrete. Every time a bad cloud came up, everyone went to the cellar.

Along in the night that summer, Joe and I decided we better take the boys and ourselves to the cellar as thunder rolled and lightning flashed across a low hanging black sky. We grabbed the boys up from their cozy bed, along with the trusted lantern. We set down on a bench to wait out the storm. I had one baby in my lap and the other one leaning against my side, half asleep. Joe sat on another bench across from us, catching a nap now and then, while I was wide awake. I wasn't too fond of those holes in the ground anyway.

When out of the blue, in a very calm voice, Joe said, "Euple, there's a big old snake just over your head."

Cutting my head around just enough to spy that slimy reptile a foot above my back, I thought I'd die with a heart attack as my heart started palpitating like a trip hammer. Jumping up with the baby, I grabbed the other one by the hand, dragging him along as best I could. I was bent on getting out of that dungeon. A storm held no fear for me under the circumstances, but that beady-eyed, tongue flickering creature did. I made a few jumps up those steps in record time, even with two babies in tow. On reaching safe ground, I sighed with relief. By that time, Joe and the trusted lantern were by our side. No amount of coaxing could make me go back in that den of snakes. For there might be more lurking around.

The storm could blow us away, but we sure weren't going to get snake bit if I could help it. If, I recall, we never went into that place again the two years we lived there. The next day, Joe took a gun down into that small chamber bent on doing away with that ugly thing. Hearing a muffled gun shot, I hoped he hit the target. Lo and behold, he came out of there with a five foot long slimy, but very dead snake. To this day I cannot tell anyone what kind of snake it was. To me, it was the enemy!

Many years later, I experienced another snake scare. We were building our present home, had all the outside walls finished and the roof on. The inside walls only had the outside boards and studs showing. A half naked façade, we had already moved into. One day in the early spring, my daughter, who was a teenager, came in the living room and calmly said, "Mama, there is a snake in my room." Rushing to see—there it was coiling itself down one of the studs. I did my famous dance as we watched its descent toward the floor. Hanging onto my daughter's arm, screeching like a demented person (her arms were sore for days). Fortunately, our teenage son was still at home, the baby boy in 1948 that I carried out of the cellar. He killed, after a wild chase, this second nightmare fifteen years later.

Some years later in my big old rambling house that was all finished now, I recall another snake story. Only this time it was a snake skin roped around a Kleenex box on top of the bathroom commode. I felt pretty smug at this time, no snakes could get inside. How wrong I was. It must have come up through the commode. I will never know. I had grandchildren at this time and one of my granddaughters came in the kitchen where I was on this particular day, and said, "Grandma, there's a snake skin in your bathroom." I laughed it off, thinking she was teasing me.

"It is, Grandma. Come and see." Sure enough, there was the proof, and I did my little scream once again.

I never found the snake that skin belonged to, thank goodness. There was a possibility it went back down the commode and out the drain. I searched every nook and cranny, so afraid I'd find it under my bed, on my bed, or in the dark closet. I never went into a dark room for many nights afterwards, for fear I would step on that slimy thing and I would die on the spot. The snake skin was all the evidence I ever found that a snake had been in my house. After many days, I was able to breath normally again.

My snake story would not be the final saga of fear without telling the tale of the Bull Frog that at the time was worse than any snake.

The summer of 1949, I was heavy with my third child in June, a month before my daughter was born. We had no cooling system at that time and as all summers in Arkansas, it was very hot and humid. I was hot, tired, half sick, and miserable, so I lay across my bed to rest for a spell. My husband had gone into the woods to hunt with his gun and dogs. All he killed was a huge bull frog. Later, coming to the house, he saw me sitting on the edge of the bed. He thought how funny it would be to throw that creature at my feet. Opening the screen door a few feet from my bed, he tossed the thing across that well worn linoleum floor and it landed at my feet. All I saw was a black slimy blur sailing across the floor directly toward me. My heart slammed against my ribcage and I fell back on the bed in a swoon. What he thought would be a hand-clapping prank turned out to be a big scare for <u>him!</u>

He fell down beside me and began to rub my face and hands, calling my name over and over, saying, "I'm sorry, Mom. Please forgive me." Forgive him—if I hadn't been pregnant, and could have gotten around better, I think I could have killed him with my bare hands, for by that time I was fighting mad.

To be sure, we didn't have fried frog legs for supper. Although I would have liked to poke that entire bug-eyed creature down Joe's throat, unskinned and uncooked. As the old timers used to believe, it's a wonder my little girl wasn't marked with a frog on her cheek.

Snakes, it seemed, found me even in church. A rubber snake Joe accidentally toss in my lap (Reflections) in the middle of church services, made me threaten to kill him in front of God and everyone.

My close encounter with the snakes and bull frog was kinda like watching a horror movie straight out of "The Black Lagoon."

Peace Be Still

Travel worn and weary
No place to lay his head
The Lord Jesus said to his disciples twelve,
"Let's go down to the seashore.
Where we'll take a boat to the other side."
While the disciples struggled at the oars,
A storm was brewing
The Lord lay sleeping in the back of the boat.
His sleep was sweet, on a pillow he lay
The fierce winds let loose its awful fury
The waves dashed high
Shaking that old boat from side to side,
The lightning flashed, the thunder rolled.
The sea went wild as it kicked up its heels.
With its screams and its squalls
Panic in their voice shaking with fear.
His disciples called out in a
voice filled with utter despair,
"Master, save us, we'll perish."
He arose at their plea, he spoke only three words that
calmed the raging sea.
Yet those three words were surging with power
that immediately took effect as he said,
"Peace be still."
I was the master of my ship, or so I thought
No one could chart the course but I
The weather was fine, not a cloud in the sky.
Smug and satisfied, I was content
to float idly and peacefully
along. No true destination in mind.
The world was mine, I began to sing a happy song.
"Sail on ol' ship, sail on."
I knew it not, but there was a
storm brewing far out at sea.
Suddenly from out of nowhere
the winds came with a shocking blow.
As the tempest tossed and the billows surged,

My ship began to rock and roll.
Anxiety, doubts and an awful fear shook my soul.
Only then did I realize I wasn't the
Master of my ship after all.
I fell to my knees, all hope was gone
Like the disciples of old, I cried out in despair,
"Master, save me lest I perish in this storm!"
From out of the tumult of the storm,
I heard the Master's voice, from
somewhere back of the boat,
calming my fearful heart.
Suddenly, all my fear was gone.
A great calm swept over the waves at sea
as I heard Him say, "Peace be still."
Are you out in the depth of the sea?
Master of your own ship, nothing to cloud your mind?
Responsibilities you've left behind?
Are you seeking the pleasures of a sinful world,
with no destination in mind?
No goals to fill while eating the bread of idleness,
and drinking the wine of plenty?
Are you riding high and dry, a soft breeze at your back,
sun shining brightly at your feet
No thought for tomorrow, you just live for today?
Be careful you don't experience a "Storm at Sea."
When the angry waves will sweep your happiness
and contentment right out to sea.
Waves of doubt and confusion will fling you to your knees,
boisterous winds will cause you to call out. Master, save me.
The Master is willing to save you for He is the
Master of all men, on land or on sea, on the mountaintop,
or in the deep. To the lost and weary, there is hope
and safety in the one who can calm any storm
That will come your way.
"Peace be Still."

Song Titles Tell a Story

A million years from now—I'm Gonna Wake Up in Glory—feeling fine—In a Mansion Next Door to Jesus—Anchored in Love Divine—Hand in Hand with Jesus—He Leadth Me—Joy Unspeakable—Heavenly Sunlight.

Ten Thousand Angels—Praise Him, Praise Him—How Great Thou Art—Glory to His Name—What a Savoir—Holy, Holy Lord God Almighty—He's Alive.

Many Miles Behind Me—Wasted Years—Amazing Grace—He Set Me Free—I Bowed on My Knees and Cried Holy, Holy—Oh, Happy Day—Love Lifted Me—Oh Say But I'm Glad—I Shall Not Be Moved—In the Sweet By and By.

I'd Rather Have Jesus—There's Sunshine in My Soul—Satisfied—Safe in the Arms of Jesus—That's Why I Love Him So—I've Never Been Sorry—I Will Sing the Wondrous Story—He Whispers Sweet Peace To Me—Swing Low Sweet Chariot, coming for to carry me home.

Lay Your Burdens Down—Tell It To Jesus—Let Jesus Come Into Your Heart—You Won't Have to Cross Jordon Alone—When The Roll Is Called Up Yonder—Farther Along—Just Beyond The Rolling River—There's A Great Day Coming.

This World is Not My Home—Some Day—After Awhile—When the Battles Are Over—It Won't Be Very Long—There is One More River to Cross—Jesus Is Coming Soon—How Beautiful Heaven Must Be—Jesus Hold My Hand—When I Wake Up To Sleep No More.

I'll Meet You in the Morning—In That City of Gold—Where The Roses Never Fade—In the Haven of Rest—There is Peace Like a River—Where We'll Never Grow Old—No Tears in Heaven—Victory in Jesus.

Camping In Cannon—With The Children of the King—On That Glad Reunion Day—Blessed Assurance—The Sweetest Name I Know—Like a Shepherd Leadth Me—In the Morning of Joy—In The Land Where Dreams Come True—Oh, For a Thousand Tongues To Sing—Ten Thousand Years Will Have Just Begun.

I would not miss it—would you?

A Taste of Stardom

Back in the early 1930's, a child star hit the movie industry, taking it by storm that made lots of bucks at the box office in Hollywood.

That little girl with short blonde hair, hanging in banana curls, was a picture of innocence and loveliness that stole the hearts of every little girl in America. She always wore a colorful, lacy, be-ribboned dress with yards of material in it and a frilly petticoat peeping out from underneath. Her attire was complete with a frilly pair of anklets and patent leather tap-dancing slippers on her feet. She sang and danced her way into stardom, under her mother's loving hand and Twentieth Century Fox.

How I longed to own a pretty white and red polka-dotted dress like hers and be able to dance as well as she could. Saturdays were the only day country kids went to the movies to see all our favorite rooting, tooting, shoot-em up cowboys riding the range on beautiful horses that knew all the tricks, due to hours of training.

Every so often a Saturday Matinee was featured on the silver screen, starring one small super star, namely, Shirley Temple. Outside of a death in the family or the car breaking down, it was a tragedy if we missed going to the show house, when she performed. Cowboys were our heroes, but Shirley Temple was our Fairy Princess.

Watching that pretty little four-year-old dancing across those shining floors of an antebellum show place, up and down a long flight of stairs, or swinging around and among those magnificent columns at the entryway was pure magic. Bo Jangles, her dancing partner was splendid in his black and white tuxedo who did his soft shoe routine as well, who never missed a beat. Together, they made an excellent couple. Every little girl memorized her song, *The Good Ship Lollipop*, and tried to mimic her voice.

Antebellum homes and chauffeur driven families were never heard of in our little neck of the woods. We were lucky if we had a broken down jalopy to ride around in. The Great Depression of 1929 had affected thousands of people all over the United States. There were many empty pockets, and very bare cupboards. Our family never actually went hungry, but there were times it was touch and go. We ate a lot of garden fare and fish.

Even in dire poverty, children dream. I dreamed of becoming another Shirley Temple as I kicked and shuffled across that old uncarpeted wooden floor in a sharecropper's cottage. With a squeaky Victrola or a battery powered static sounding radio to dance to. I say danced! It was a matter of jumping and shuffling in my case, for I never mastered the art of tap-dancing. Those old floors jumped and squeaked loudly under my feet for months before I realized I could never be another Shirley Temple. My dancing career died before it really started as well as my childish dreams.

Yet I learned from the tender age of six years, when I started to school, I could sing fairly well from all the singing games we played. There was *London Bridge is Falling Down, Hi Ho the Derry-O, Old MacDonald, Here We Go Around the Mulberry Bush.* We even sang a jolly tune when we jumped rope or played hop-scotch.

Up to almost eight decades I've had a song in my heart that carried me through childhood, through the hurdles of a teenager, into the life and joys of a wife, mother, grandmother and great-grandmother. Yet those years were often wrought with heartache and tears as well.

No, I never hit the big time in the music field, never sang for a vast audience, yet I never lost my first love, or that first peep into the singing world of one little starlet from Tinsel Town. Even so, I've always had a select group of people. I performed for my family and close friends. My well-known Play House was known as a "Field of Dreams," located on Moore House Road. My voice often vibrated over the big cathedral in the sky. My opening night was on an outdoor pavilion, garnished with a profusion of stars. My greatest achievement was in a small but well-established church in the wildwood. My greatest thrill was singing an Irish lullaby to my infant listeners as my voice caught and held throughout the portals of *This Old House.*

My greatest fan was the man of my dreams, who attended every performance I ever made for 47 years until he made his debut in the cathedral in the sky. I do believe it was yours truly who made *You Are My Sunshine,* famous over the hills of Arkansas.

It has been said *Love is a Many Splendored Thing.* I believe a singing heart can be characterized as such, for as a teenager, I joyously belted out *The Yellow Rose of Texas, Frankie and Johnny, On Top of Ol' Smokey, Beautiful Dreamer, She'll Be Coming Around the Mountain, My Blue Heaven, Home on the Range,* and others. *Wabash Cannonball* could be heard floating over the countryside for miles for I had a voice that eventually called the cows from the back forty, a mile away.

When I grew older and became a minister's wife, my favorite songs became *the* songs of Zion. Riney Hill flowed under *How Great Thou Art, Amazing Grace, When We All Get To Heaven, Swing Low Sweet Chariot, He Set Me Free,* and *Blessed Assurance.* Those were just a few of the many I sang daily and at church on the weekend. Yesterday and today, those old favorites were and are my lifeline to *Heavens Jubilee,* where there will always be a song.

Remembering the little Hollywood starlet, I believe she was one who helped put the toe-tapping rhythm in my feet, and the love of music and song in my heart. That little girl grew up and went on to better and higher things according to the magazines and newspapers I hoarded for years. It took years for me to lose my fascination for the small, renowned child who later became Mrs. Shirley Black. As for me I became a star in my own right, brought up under the tutorship of a loving family. At the age of 18, I took up the duties of a wife and the greatest profession of all—a mother. Second on my list of achievements was being a minister's help mate. My spouse and I worked tirelessly together for many years for the betterment of life.

My own five children often had country soil on their legs and bare feet, sprinkled in their hair, with mud covered playhouse hands as they traced patterns of muck all over their cherub features. Mama only saw beauty as she stole a kiss or two from those grubby little cheeks. Oh, well. It was easy to wash away at days end. Yet, a tired worn out mother was glad when her five little tousled heads hit the sack. Many nights we were all too tired to repeat our nightly prayer; *Now I lay me down to sleep, I pray the Lord my soul to keep.*

Lulled to sleep under mama's song, all was well as, "Good night, children," lingered in their ears long after sleep overcame them. Knowing mama and daddy was nearby and they were safe and protected in their little world.

Going back to the days of childhood, movies and child stars, I have since learned it is not money and prestige that makes the world go round. I can wear my inexpensive wardrobe with pride and still be happy. I am content standing in my farm kitchen munching on a slice of cornbread smeared with a gob of margarine as any well-to-do person feasting on all sorts of exotic food. Peanut butter, cheese and crackers are just as good today as it was seventy years ago in a sharecropper's cottage. Looking into the faces of all the rich and famous, there is heartache and trouble in their world and they are often unhappy. I'm thankful I can go to the supermarket today and be able to load up a cart piled high with all sorts of food, but I feel sorry for the rich, who never wore homemade clothes that were often patched and faded. Yet a lot of love was added to every stitch and fold. Our world was safe from crime, homeless children and child molesters.

Rich kids never had the luxury of going barefoot all summer or splashing around in a small inlet cove at the edge of a small island retreat where my family and I lived. Never felt sweet music rippling through the waist high wild grass, swaying in the breeze. Most of the rich were town folks, whose children wore shoes to protect their feet from the heat radiating from the hot pavement of city streets. We had something else Hollywood and other big cities didn't have, our little Island of Paradise embraced by the mighty Mississippi River, kicking up its mighty heels day after day along its boundaries, where cotton was King, while Ol' Man River just kept rolling along. Children, who were raised with a silver spoon in their mouth, were never lulled to sleep by the frog choir, or the whippoorwill's song while they hid among the canebrakes and cattails. The lyrics of the river breeze was like no other as it scampered among the huge trees— whistling in and out among the ghostly cypress knees, standing at attention like so many stone face carvings. Oh, yes, it was an ideal performance with a Hawaiian flair, with dozens of phantom dangers, swaying around in slimy grass skirts on a hand swept sandy beach.

I can still hear the huge bull frogs and the small toads coming out to play nightly, adding their mating call to the symphony from the top of a colorful lily pad. His reward was a slimy caress. Tug boats made their way down river each day, carrying precious cargo to the big city, yodeled a working crew's ballad. Crossing the Mississippi on a slow ferry boat as a child was 4th of July, birthdays, and Christmas all rolled into one. My favorite pirate, Captain Hook and I were riding the high sea together and I believe I heard his evil laughter. Nights along the river, the star's shone brighter as they glittered and danced among its watery image. The moon saw its reflection in the mirrored depths all night. The scent of wild flowers blended into the smells of spring, deliciously tickling the nose with a fragrance of perfume and wild roses. Oh, yes, life on our little oasis was every fisherman's dream. It was like a day at the fish market, where one could pick and choose his or her catch. Preferably, the big old catfish ruled the dinner table.

Do you suppose a child from Hollywood ever walked inside a riverboat nestled near a tree-lined moss covered bank? Where fresh fish was the main course at supper time and in between? Fireflies to light up the night skies as crickets and katydids performed on cue. There was always a band of chirring birds and wild geese honking their way down river. A pair of hoot owls raised their voices in defiance of losing a meal, as a lone deer and its baby loped alongside, was a refreshing picture to go to sleep on.

A lone hobo working his way down river to places unknown, with maybe a few pennies in his pocket, a change of clothes and a cooking pot and pan in a small bundle slung on his shoulder, chanting a "Happy Drifter's" lament: *Yonder comes a man with a sack on his back, honey. Yonder comes a man with sack on his back, babe. Yonder comes a man with a sack on his back, he's got more crawdads than he can pack, honey, baby mine.*

Our little world was not always so picture perfect when the dreaded water moccasins invaded our little garden of Eden with their slimy treacherous bodies undulating across one's path, curled around a cypress knee or peeked out from underneath a rotting log, spitting out its poisonous tongue in rebellion, traced back to when it deceived Eve into eating the forbidden fruit in the renowned Garden of Eden.

A sharecropper's lot belonged to hundreds of people in the 1930's, especially where cotton was King. Kids that grew up in a cotton patch were as loved and cared for as any well-to-do children, for our homes were always chocked full of love and thrived under a peaceful atmosphere. I never felt deprived of those two elements of parental affection.

Even so, we had no time clocks to punch or schedule to keep. We were never too busy to visit a sick neighbor and give them a helping hand. A promised word was an honest man's Bible. We were never so over-worked that we couldn't take a day or even two to celebrate an important holiday or just have old fashioned fun. Born with a cotton sack on your back, if you had a little nest egg laid back—with a running car to drive—you could hob-nob with the well-to-do. Landlords were called Mr. and Mrs., otherwise you were known as old man and his old lady So and So living on Mr. Moore's place. Not that we had it much better than thousands of others did, but my Dad could always pull a rabbit out of the hat so to speak, when funds ran low. He was a well-liked hard-working man that was admired and respected. He was also one of the few low paid farmers who were called Mr. Tutt by everyone. It was men like my Daddy who was called The Salt of the Earth.

The well-heeled landlords and the wealthy businessmen were far too busy taking care of their abundant holdings to enjoy the simplicity of life as we knew it—so I ask in all sincerity— who had the best of two worlds?

Some of Life's Bitter Moments

Chickens ran loose in the yard back in the good ole days. Fences were only for animals. It wasn't always easy to side-step a big gob of chicken poop with that squishy, slimy mess all over your feet and in between your toes, as often was the case of being barefoot. Children wore no shoes from the first of May (or that was my schedule) until it got too cold late in the fall. Children didn't have access to a modern bathtub, so we wiped it off on a patch of grass, or in a chicken wallow full of dirt. If a child had on their shoes it was often tracked into the house on freshly scrubbed wooden floors. Of course, said child was booted out of the house and told to go to the pump and wash their shoes off. To us kids, what did a little chicken poop matter? It didn't bother us near as much as it did our nicey nice parents.

After the water was applied, we didn't dare wear shoes back in the house for the smell lingered, until maybe one stepped in another pile. Did you ever smell fresh chicken poop? It's a scent one doesn't want to carry around. If chickens were as big as pigs, we would have had a world wide catastrophe, for there is no smell like hog leavings. That smell lingers for miles across country. The scent is a nose holder, an eye-popping stink, coming from the fumes that dance up your nose and almost suffocates you. I wonder why somebody hasn't invented "Hog Poop Deodorant."

Yet when one of those lard rolling critters look up at you with those big brown eyes as they grunt a happy hello at you, the situation was reviewed and you sort of ignored the smell. One fell in love with a four-legged mud slinging, hoggy creature with seven or eight roly-poly babies lagging along behind, begging for dinner.

Ah, yes. Those with a sensitive nose or a weak stomach had better stay far away from a hog farm. Let the old seasoned farmer with hog perfume up his nose, drunk on swill, wearing overalls and rubber boots accommodate seven hundred pounds of pork. Slurping slop and gobbling dried corn. Ain't that just like a pig?

At least they didn't try to suck the life blood out of you when you approached them like the dreaded bed bugs did. A whole squadron of bed bug recruits attacked at night as they silently crawled out of the woodwork, bent on revenge and mayhem, seeking anyone they could dine on. The only way the family could roust them (there was no remedy for bed bugs at the stores) was to saturate a rag in kerosene and rub it all over the mattress and the folds around the edge, and set the four legs in a container of kerosene. It wouldn't kill them; it only ran them away, hiding once again in the walls and cracks. Those old houses had lots of hiding places as they bid their time until the housekeeper forgot her weekly chore. They were hungrier than ever and you learned a hard lesson if you forgot to spike the bed.

In the late 1930's and early 1940's, DDT and other insecticides come on the market that killed the little blood sucking pests. It was so good slipping into sun dried sheets and get a good night's sleep without breathing kerosene fumes. "Who needed cinch bugs, anyway?"

I never heard of, nor saw a tick until we moved to Randolph County in 1940. I was fourteen years old and starting a new school. I was a little apprehensive about being the new kid on the block. But I was well received and soon fit right in. A group of us girls were sitting on the school grounds having a gab fest. All at once, I felt something crawling up my leg. Looking down, I saw this funny looking bug crawling toward my upper body, lickety split. You would have thought the world was coming to an end the way I carried on. Snakes and spiders were my mortal enemies. From that day on, ticks were added to the list. The girl's laughed at me and said, "It's only a tick." Only a tick? How could anything that little crawl so fast and look so big? Nothing had prepared me for that dreaded blood hungry parasite. In a voice filled with fright, I said, "Get it off me. Get it off me." After a few minutes, I realized it was me screaming those terrifying words. One of the girls casually reached over and picked it off me and killed it. That was my first lesson in tick anthology.

During those former years, we had no Hot Shot or Off, to keep the dreaded mosquitoes at bay. When they came, they came to stay. They wined and dined us all night long, while serenading us with a nerve grating lullaby. Then they would hole up in some cozy spot and sleep all day. You would think the way we slapped them around, they would realize they were unwanted guests and leave. But no, they were more determined than ever to hang around the banquet table, lapping up all the available food with their razor sharp needle beaks.

Mosquitoes were a nuisance by night and flies by day. They swarmed all over the house and ate out of left over crusty pots and pans and they even had the gall to want to eat out of your plate at mealtimes. They played hop-scotch on the wall, floors and the ceiling. Humans were their playground. They tickled your nose and danced over every exposed part of your body. Busy as they were, they still had time to buzz your number.

We had no such convenience as *OFF* or any other bug spray. You accepted your lifestyle as it was (insecticide was unknown). Fly swatters were not invented. We had to keep the wooden door closed so we didn't stay indoors very much on hot summer days. Cardboard fans or an outdoor breeze was our cooling system. Babies slept under a covering of netting to protect them.

Such was the good ole days. Who wants to go back to that???

My Spiritual House

When the unclean spirit is gone out of man, he walketh through dry places, seeking rest and finding none. Then he saith, I will return unto my house from which I came and when he findeth it empty swept and garnished then goeth he and taketh with himself seven other spirits more wicked than himself and they enter in and dwell there, and the last state of that man is worse than the first. Even so shall it be also unto this wicked generation. Matt: 12:43-45

Reading those words, I was reminded of homemakers around the world, cleaning house. Then I was reminded of Christian homemakers, keeping a "Spiritual House." If our own spiritual house is getting coated over with old forgotten sins, it's time to start house cleaning.

What better place to start than in the kitchen of dissatisfaction? Let's throw out all the scraps of despair. Wash all the crusty plates of discontent. Cook up a savory dish of happiness. The aroma of sweetness will fill the air and others will be drawn to its source. Throw all the stained curtains of selfishness into the washer of goodness. Clean the table of impatience and cover it with a pretty tablecloth of cheerfulness. Prepare a centerpiece with a bouquet of joy and beauty. Wash the ceiling of unhappiness; cover it with a paint of gladness. Scrub down the walls of anger with a thick layer of laughter. Use a bucket of sunshine and the mop of kindness on the floors of heartache and tears.

Moving on to the bedrooms, straighten up the bed of chaos and disorder; sleep the sleep of trust and confidence. Dig out the closet of junk stored away out of sight, such as gossip, back biting, ignorance, pride, and self-righteousness. Probably hidden away far back on the back shelf is a box of pretense. Try using a gallon or two of honesty and pretense will disappear immediately. Could there be a dirty old gob of hatefulness setting just inside the closet door? Throw it out, and replace it with a box of tenderness. Lastly, dust and vacuum the floors with a song of magic.

Right next to the bedroom is the bathroom. Use a sponge of gentleness on the mildew of jealousy with the help of Mr. Clean. Distrust can be flushed down the drain. When you finish with that, even the crud can become The Shining. Shine the mirror of haughtiness with a song of hope. Clean out the waste basket of discarded leftovers, line it with cheer. Clean the floor with magic carpet.

Suppose unexpected company drops in? Do you suddenly sweep those secret sins under the rug, such as laziness, envy, resentment, dislike? Or perhaps you swept that little fit you just had a few minutes before under the rug out of sight. No one must know you lost your temper.

Or you can greet them with a welcome smile of good things to come. Such as a lavish helping of good fortune, and a refreshing drink from your fountain of success. Lavishly use the dust cloth of beauty, which will rid your house of the cobwebs of ugliness. The dust and grime of bitterness will disappear with smiles and contentment. A bottle of love will clean the film of half truths from the windows, known as fibs. Shine them with a cloth of honesty. Forgiveness is also a good cleanser. Looking through the windows of clarity, perhaps you can reach out a helping hand to another struggling housekeeper.

Now that we have thoroughly cleaned our house, it's time to take off that old dirty coat of depression, bathe out the grime of frustration and shampoo with devotion. Brush out the tangles of indifference, spray each lock with concern. Put on a clean garment of understanding. Fill your pockets full of love and happiness, top it off with a smile, and give them away to all you meet. Put on a comfortable pair of shoes, polished with praise and thanksgiving.

Now it seems as if everything is under control. Clean house, clean person, clean heart. It's time to relax and set down on the couch of apathy and take a nap. Not so. There is one thing lacking yet. The most important. Pick up the Book of Life and read it with delight and inspiration for it has the words of hope and relaxation, giving you wisdom and knowledge. It is a store house of courage, strength, protection and peace in times of need.

Now with a song in your heart and a lighter step in your feet, it's time to visit the "Spiritual Dwelling" at the House of Prayers.

Hillbilly Jargon

Here is some hillbilly jargon for you to chew on. Hope it doesn't stick in your craw or curdle your mind. You can call it mountain music slightly off-key with a southern dialect to it. We often get our tang tongueled up and it comes out like a lot of gobbly-d gook. You can say I've been up the river a few times without a paddle. Through the death of my better half, I learned to paddle my own canoe and hoe my own row. I've even stumbled over my own feet, been cut down to size, and blew my own horn for almost four score years. I've loved and raised five healthy, rambunctious children. Laughed with my fun-loving bed and breakfast partner, I tied the knot with sixty years ago this spring. Through thick and thin, we stuck together like hot molasses on corn bread for forty-seven-years. The tales he told tickled our funny bone and kept us in stitches. Ah, yes, he was a barrel of monkeys. Every so often his jokes backfired on him, and the kids and I wanted to shoot-a-monkey. I've kissed a monkey's uncle and I'll probably look like a monkey when I grow old.

We didn't have much moola and we often had to pull ourselves up by the boot straps. Our clothes were often work-worn and patched, but we were quite content living way down on the farm among the mooing, neighing, squealing, bleating, crowing, clucking, quacking, gobbling, barking, meowing, and kids caterwauling. We were as slap happy as seven pigs wallowing around in a mud hole. Our little whippersnappers looked like they had taken a mud bath at the end of the day. Torn clothing with mud in their hair, they were pint-sized angels in disguise, without wings, of course. Mama called them her little ragamuffins and when our young'uns failed to tote their end of the load, I always told them to lick their calf over. We wondered why they were so put out with those words of wisdom. By golly and by gosh, they had druther kiss a bullfrog.

I guess you could say I'm a tough old bird who counted her chickens before they hatched, but I never put all my eggs in one basket. I saved some for a rainy day. Many rainy days have since fallen and I'm too old to make sweet music with a new grandpa. We couldn't cut a rug together anyway.

115

Our two sons were as close as two peas in a pod. Together they could fight a circle saw at the drop of a hat. They were always trying out their skills as a cowpoke, always horsing around. One day they stirred up some angry bees that took the cat-a-wampus out of them. Talk about doing the twist. Wasn't that a windinger? Their daddy, who was a robber stopper of stinger-bingers, thought that was a honey of a deal, for he always had a sweet tooth.

My first born was always falling out of, or into something. One fatal day, he fell off his horse and broke his what'cha ma callit and skint his somewhat. The saw bones said he broke his femur. That was a 'furrin" word for us Arkansas cotton pickers. We thought he broke his leg. Two months later he came home with a gimp in his get along. The girls all swarmed around him like bees in a hive. He grabbed a smoke he kept for just such an emergency that had a calming affect on all the little honey bees. When the smoke cleared, his brother grabbed him a little honeycomb too. If those two wasn't a cat's Aunt Jane. I guess you could say they had a bee in their bonnets. Our three girls are pretty as a picture, sharp as a tack, raised on razorblade soup, fashioned with new nails. "Ellie Mae gone to Hollywood never looked so good!" The boys flocked around them like flies. But believe me, there were no flies on those three. Their weapons were candy on a stick. If that didn't work, crocodile tears did. They were so sweet, sugar wouldn't melt in their mouth.

Take a gander at this juicy tidbit; the old Bozo who lives down on Hoot and Hollow loves to guzzle his white lightning, that will curl ones hair and sizzle your toe nails. He was higher than a kite, soused like an old wet hen, meaner than a wall-eyed pole cat (skunk). He always smells like one, too. One day last week, the neighbors heard him flailing the tar out of his wife. It seems she set him off by feeding him pickles and sour grapes. A few more wouldn't matter since he was as pickled as a cucumber himself.

Ah, the girl next door is as pretty as a speckled pup, but she doesn't have a lick of horse sense. Take last month for instance. She was so bum-fuzzled she spit on a house fire and called for help. Her tongue got in front of her eyeteeth and she couldn't see what she was saying. She said she couldn't walk for she had a bone in her leg. It seems she doesn't have a leg to stand on anyway. Well, jump up and sit down, that's what I call a pea brain.

My daddy, a widower, was a Yankee-doodle dandy who liked to spruce up for a night on the town. He wore a new well-shaped hat, cocked just so over one eye, wearing a white starched shirt, complete with a snazzy necktie around his Adam's apple and a knife edge crease down both legs of his pants, with a white handkerchief tucked in his coat pocket. Shoes shined to the hilt that he could see his face in, smelling of talcum powder, shaving soap and bay rum hair tonic. Jumping Jehoshophat he was as clean as a whistle, cocky as a banty rooster. Ah, yes, my brother, sister and I knew he was a hep cat; the cat's meow.

In recent years, I've developed a pain in my get along, my hearing is shot, I drool in my sleep and I have snow on the mountain. Every night I take my thing-a-ma-gig off and place it on a shelf. My get up and go has got up and went. I'm left feeling a little frazzled as this jalopy has about run out of gas. If you're hungry as a bear looking for something to stick to your ribs, come on to my house. You'll probably find me busy as a bee, biling dem cabbages down, cooking corn pone and fat back. But if you'd ruther, I'll serve up some hot homemade biscuits slathered with lick-um dab (gravy) that will make you want to slap your mama. Now ain't that a jaw breaker? Or I'll fry up a skillet of pig strips and all the hen fruit you can eat. I'll brew up a pot of hot java and all the squeeze juice you can drink. I assure you they will be vituals that will melt in your mouth, honey chile, known as slap-luscious and larruping good. Talk about eating high on the hog. My famous fried chocolate pies, fresh apple cake, and candied yams will satisfy your sweet tooth.

For thirteen years, my sweet petunia is eating pie in the sky. My chickens flew the coop many moons ago. Still them and their young fryers often come home to roost. That warms the cockles of my heart. Well, shut my mouth if that doesn't beat a hen-a-pecking, or the old red rooster who lost his scratch. Without his scratch, he couldn't feed bugs and worms to his clucks. Talk about chickens, I bet you didn't know I discovered the goose who laid the golden egg down on 2353 Washington Road in my little rook on the hill.

Ya'll come back, you heah?

The Party

Seeing a herd of cows under a shade tree in an open pasture sparked this tale. A cow tale that is.

The party was held in #1 Pasture on Shade Tree Hill, right next door to Pond. It was an ideal place for a bovine party, under the spreading branches of a huge oak tree.

Mrs. Bossy and Mrs. Jersey was in charge of all the eats and arrangements (Hostesses of the week). According to Mrs. Bossy, who was a native of Wyoming, the party theme should be "Green Grass of Wyoming." All the side dishes were flavored with green mint, party favors were varied colors of green. Green place mats for the ladies and children. The tableland was decorated with greenery, a green carpet was spread out over the outdoor pavilion, spotted here and there with big brown moldy piles of residue left over from the last get together. There was green cuisine catered from Northeast Arkansas, located west of Riceland at the "Eatry" off Current River where the scent tickled your nose. The drinks were spiked with green algae from the huge reservoir on Pond. One of the matriarchs of the herd snitched some green corn cobs for dessert, just across the fence in the farmer's field, or what they could reach by stretching their necks a bit. (The farmer would never miss them anyway.)

All the guests were dressed to kill. Mrs. Bossy was wearing a brown and white outfit, while Mrs. Jersey was wearing a shimmering golden yellow creation, a well-known designer made just for her. Young Miss Blackie was showing off a dazzling black gown, suitable for a Queen. She was sure to catch the eyes of a young male she had her eye on. Mrs. Holstein was a huge, good-looking dame, parading around in a white and black suit. To show off her attire, she sashayed across everyone's vision to plant a wet kiss on her offspring, "Babe," who was her pride and joy. Babe was the best dressed youngster in the group, wearing white moo-hair, complete with black dancing shoes.

Then there was Grandma Daisy. She had birthed too many children to worry about her appearance. Too many seasons had come and gone and she was feeling her age. It didn't matter if her dress wasn't too clean, and had seen better days. She felt like she had earned a rest from her labors, as she lolled around on the green turf, calmly chewing on a mouthful of choice tidbits. Little Bit had not bothered to fancy up either, for her life was full of bumps and bruises. Being an orphan, she was always run off from the food that left her lean and hungry. Then there was Blaze, known by the white stripe down the center of her face. She was an amazon type of a gal, wearing a marvel of cream and tan, only a Queen would wear. After all, she was a dairy man's dream, a heavy milker and a breeder of pure bred stock. Mr. Bull (his master had called him Jr. ever since he was a young steer), was milling around among the young ladies. They thought he was a handsome devil wearing his gleaming sand toned dinner jacket. He had his eyes on two willing young heifers that suited his fancy. They were about the prettiest little things cavorting all over the place in their finery. Sidling up to one of them, he scented her intoxicating perfume, inviting him to nuzzle her neck. Here was a conquest no healthy male could pass up. Jr. was the man of the hour; he took no nonsense off his huge harem. Mrs. Gert, one of his former lovers was casting him a wicked eye as she watched his performance with the brazen young things. She let out a bellow of rage at their lack of decorum—"For shame!"

Some of the teenagers were doing some fancy foot work across the green carpet, as Miss Betsy, the vocalist of the herd belted out her rendition of "Sweet Betsy From Pike." All the others joined in, and their voices rang out over the countryside in harmony with nature. Thanks to Mrs. Bossy and Mrs. Jersey, the party was a success. Everyone had gorged themselves until they could not eat another morsel.

Little Bit won the door prize, a year's supply of grain. She was in calf heaven, savoring her hour of triumph. Later in the afternoon, all the babies were off playing hide and seek or chasing butterflies, so the womenfolk settled down for a gab fest, mostly about the two-legged creatures that ran the farm. "Farmer Joe is a pretty good vet; he takes good care of us. He pours that vile tasting medicine down our throat or gives us a shot when we are sick. That makes us better, even if we do hate it. The boss's wife is a loving, generous soul," said Mrs. Sadie, "she is always telling me what a fine milk cow I am, as she strokes my neck and back."

"Ah, yes, I remember one cold morning I kicked the bucket out of my mistress's hands, splattering milk all over her. Afterward, I was sorry for my behavior, but the pain she inflicted on my sore bag was terrible. After that she smoothed some healing ointment on me."

"I hate that noisy old rooster, who wakes us every morning before daylight," Grandma Daisy said, "With this cockle-doodle-do lingo. What's so important about rise and shine at four o'clock in the morning? I think I'd relish human food if that old rascal wound up in a chicken pot pie."

"Look at the uppity Mrs. Hereford, standing over there alone. She curls up her lip at all of us country bumpkins, coming from a distant land and all. Always showing off her beautiful red coat. It's rumored she has a pedigree and her blood lines go back to the dark ages it seems. What makes her think she is so important? She landed on the same turf as we are," said Miss Sissy.

Miss Bessie, a wiser old head, said, "Oh, well, it's something we have to expect when we get one of those damsels from a "Big Farm," out in the country.

And the conversation went on as the sun slowly sank into the west. All too soon, they heard the farmer calling suppertime. Rounding up all the stragglers, they meandered slowly toward the barn yard. Mothers pushed their reluctant bawling children onward. With a switch of their tails at a horde of horseflies, they lumbered down a well-worn path toward their sanctuary – The Lazy R.

Dad's Cows

I

I was thrust out into the world on a warm, balmy day on May 10, 2003, through no fault of my own. With no rhyme or reason other than to captivate others as the world sought my eloquence.

Carefree and drifting with no place to call my own, my feet caught the wanderlust bug. So saying, I proceeded to set out on an unforgettable journey. At times my equilibrium wasn't so good; I was down more than I was up. Strangely enough, there were times I could pivot across the world's stage in a ballerina pose. With no sense of direction, or destination in mind, like a thistle blowing in the wind, I had no roots or stability to hold me down. In my haste and folly, I soared merrily along down a county road. I did not know where life was taking me, nor did I care.

Young as I was with no experience, I knew very little of the ways of the world, so I drifted along without fear of the unknown. I was content to drift along, stopping now and then to view the beauty I encountered. A beautiful blue sky overhead. A glowing sunrise, a pretty rainbow arching across the universe, children at play, roses in bloom. A golden field of waving grain. Resting for a spell, I stopped to admire a stately oak tree. Looking up at its magnificent splendor, I decided to dwell awhile in its cooling shade. Moving on, I passed a farmhouse where I encountered a huge barking dog that proceeded to paw me around. Eluding his clutches, I scampered up a tree, cowering there in fright. At last the dog grew tired of the game and moved on. Taking heart, I ran away across an open meadow strewn with wildflowers with their fragrance lingering in the air. I pushed on. Hearing a bird serenading his mate, I stopped to listen and was reminded of *Love's Old Sweet Song*. His only audience was his mate and I. Passing a loving home, I heard a mother singing a small child a lullaby. One day a pretty little blonde girl came out to play, bringing with her a brand new baby doll dressed all in satin and lace, laying it in my embrace. The next day, she threw me away, robbing me of a joy I had never known. Trying to drown my sorrow, I took wing across a babbling brook where a little boy sat on its bank, holding a fishing pole in his hands, with a can of worms at his feet.

Early one morning, I strolled by a big, beautiful edifice. The sign outside said, "Good morning. Come join us in church today." Church was not in my vocabulary, but I decided to set a spell and listen. Sweet music flowed from its confines, and I heard a booming voice talking about a good man called Jesus. Edging closer, I heard him tell how some wicked men had beaten Him, hanging Him on a huge wooden cross where they left him to die. Born in a lowly stable, like me, he had no place to call His own, yet He was willing to suffer at the hands of his enemy. His only crime was seeking justice and equality for all mankind. Hatred placed Him there on a lonely hilltop called Mount Calvary. Bloody and bruised, wearing a crown of thorns mockers had placed on His head. Groaning in agony, His final words were, "Father, forgive them, for they know not what they do." My robe was stained with tears for the man called Jesus as I turned to leave. With the wind urging me to move on, I was soon out of hearing distance. In another time and another place, I would have covered Him from the cold and elements.

Storm clouds began to gather. As it began to rain, I sought cover under a huge boulder where I stayed nice and dry throughout the storm. As the thunder boomed, I was reminded of the day that Jesus died and I trembled with fear.

The sun was shining brightly in my face when I awoke. Mr. Wind whistled from above, urging me to follow him, saying, "Come, go with me, and you will see the world at a much faster pace." Having an adventurous heart, I followed his path. His wind song rose to heights I have never heard, as we danced and cavorted all over our oasis, sometimes high above the trees, like a kite in the sky. At other times, Mr. Wind sang a gentle song and we skipped along at ground level. As the sun began to sink slowly in the west, my friend blew himself out, leaving me stranded on a lonely vine covered hillside, covered with brambles and thistles to hover close to the ground, all alone in the dark. My rest was troubled as I tossed and turned throughout the night.

Sluggish and tired at the break of dawn, I viewed my appearance with distaste. A strong, musty smell permeated from my façade and I saw my once new outfit was dirty, stained and wrinkled almost beyond repair. In fact, I was a mess. Somewhere along the way, I realized age was catching up with me, and I was tired. At last I knew life was not always fun and games. Travel worn and weary, I noticed my frame was shrinking and wear and tear had corroded my profile. I began to wonder what was to be my destiny? My journey had taken me many miles over hills and plains, over small branches and muddy terrain, across busy shopping malls and bypassed many homes. In my hey-day, I heard music and danced to the drumbeat of time. Once I sped by a speeding train and heard its lonely whistle whine. I barely escaped with my life one day as I blew into town up next to a dirty old trash bin, where I would have been crushed to death under all that garbage and filth.

Seeking youth and adventure had led me down a long path I no longer wanted to travel. Struggling along in my misery like a tired old soldier, I was beat. Meandering down a country road, I discovered a beautiful garden setting, abundant with lovely flowers, well trimmed shrubbery and noble trees full of warbling birds. I thought perhaps I could spend my remaining days in this beautiful spot. However, the next morning, the gardener picked me up roughly with a gloved hand along with other debris, and I was thrown on a bon-fire nearby, where I quickly went up in smoke.

Many miles across town, a young lady was looking for an article she saw that she wanted to keep from the front page of the Daily Chronicle, published May 10, 2003. Searching high and low, it was nowhere to be found.

The moral of this story is—a newspaper should never lose sight of its guideline.

Aunt Naomi

No one ever called her Naomi. It was always Nomie to all her friends and family. Young as I was, I never knew the difference, she was just Aunt Nomie to me and I adored her. She took me under her wing when my mother died in 1927, two years after I was born.

My Dad, big brother, sister and I lived just down the road a piece from Aunt Nomie and her family. I was at their house almost as much as I was at home. Going to their house was a fun thing, and I gloried in all the attention I got. It was a heady feeling—for it was always, "Poor little motherless, Euple." They never got beyond calling me Little Euple even when I grew up. I thought I was one fortunate little girl to have two families, and two homes. If I cried, there was someone to comfort me. When I was sick, Aunt Nomie and my big sister were my nurses.

Mary, Aunt Nomie's youngest daughter was four years older than I and my playmate. Ah, yes, I had the best of two worlds, or so I thought. Until 1937, at the age of eleven years, my world came crashing down, when Aunt Nomie and her family left Missouri, our home state and moved to California.

California in the 1930's was a world away. I just knew I would never see my second family ever again. I cried for weeks. In my innocence, I could not imagine why they had to go away and leave me. Yet there was no way I could leave my own family to go with them. My childhood prediction almost came true, I only saw my precious Aunt Nomie one time afterward—when she came for a short visit in the late 1940's, after I had grown up and married.

Although we were miles apart, Aunt Nomie never forgot her Little Euple. The miles never lessoned her love. She kept me in touch with her family regularly. As long as she lived, she remembered every birthday, my courtship and marriage, the birth of my five children and all the years in between. Boxes of clothes and toys for the children came often. Letters and pictures of her family came at least once a month. Even so, most of the family I've never seen—though through the many pictures I received, I felt the kinship from the youngest to the oldest.

In 1966, Aunt Nomie took sick and died, leaving a heart broken family, me included. Even in her final moments, she was thinking of me, for she had packed a box addressed to Mrs. Euple Riney. She never forgot the little girl she left behind so many years ago. I shall always carry the image of a mother's love as I think of Aunt Nomie.

Mary, her youngest daughter, took over the letter writing where Aunt Nomie left off, sending me many pictures, until she too, died in the later part of the 1980's, breaking all contact with the family.

Until 2005 when we located Mike, Mary's son through the internet. A phone call was all it took to bring my family back. What a thrill it was to hear her son's voice, as he brought me up to date on the family's whereabouts. Aunt Nomie was never satisfied without the presence of children around her. Some years ago, she had adopted Wanda, one of her granddaughters. I had no clue what her married name was. Through Mike, I learned she lived in the same town, a few blocks from him.

My story does not end here I'm happy to say. In the summer of 2006, I got a phone call from Wanda, the little girl I had not seen since she was a little over a year old. She told me she and her husband were coming to Arkansas to see me. Ah, the joy of seeing her and her husband. The tie that binds was still there after seventy years.

We had so many years to catch up on. We talked continually the three days they were here. We not only talked, we held each other and cried an ocean of tears. At other times we laughed at little tid-bits of information. It was a joy to share in the life of the woman we all loved. As we reminisced, of days of old, it was as if the years rolled away and we were children again. The tears flowed freely one last time peppered with hugs and kisses as they left for home and I wondered once again, at my age, would I ever see them again?

Wanda not only left me beautiful memories, she left me a gift that belonged to Aunt Nomie. A beautiful gold plated necklace and earrings to match embedded with glass stones called Aurora Borealis. It has to be at least forty-five or fifty years old, for Aunt Nomie has been gone forty years. Yet it still gleams its magic, in all its shining splendor in its original box. Of course, I cried all over again.

It is an inexpensive piece of costume jewelry, but to me they are diamonds that were once worn by a Golden Lady, called Aunt Nomie. Each time that I wear it, I feel her embrace and I sense I hear a soft voice whispering in my ear, "I love you, Little Euple."

And like the Northern Lights, Aunt Nomie will glow in my memory forever.

Euple's Aunt Naomi

Whatever Happened to the Classics and the Nursery Rhymes?

Dear Queen of Hearts: I have been scanning *Gulliver's Travels* and I see, to appease his hunger, *Robinson Crusoe* ate Pease porridge hot, Pease porridge cold, nine days old, while he pined for *My Bonnie Lies Over the Ocean.*

The Grapes of Wrath ran freely during the *Gold Rush, Old Yeller* chased *The Yearling* through the woods and Over the Hill to Grandma's House. *Cinderella* lived happily ever after with her Boy Prince in King Edward's Court. Old shep frightened the cow who jumped over the moon that splattered *Humpety Dumpety. The Swiss Family Robinson* lived on an island where ships passed in the night. *White Fang* dreamed of living on the open plains to romp and play with the children who lived in *The Little House on the Prairie. Thunderhead* ran away with *Black Beauty,* but wound up with *My Friend Flicka.*

Twenty Thousand Leagues Under the Sea lives *The Little Mermaid* with *A Fish Called Wanda. To Kill a Mockingbird* deserves *Crime and Punishment. Little Boy Blue* fell asleep under the haystack to hide from *Baa Baa Black Sheep.* Little Miss Muffet was frightened by *The Itsy Bitsy Spider.*

Alice in Wonderland dined out in the hole in the wall with Peter Cottontail. The little *Gingerbread Man* ran away from *Hansel and Gretel. The Good Earth* was far away from *The Old Man and The Sea. The Cross and the Switchblade* struck fear in the brave heart of *Ivanhoe. Braveheart* had to run to his rescue.

Goldilocks ate all the alphabet soup of *The Three Bears* in the *Little House in the Woods. The Three Little Pigs* heard *The Call of the Wild* and dined on boiled wolf stew. Hiawatha committed a crime when he kidnapped Minnehaha. *Beauty and the Beast* discovered *The Golden Fleece. Huckleberry Finn* spit and chewed all the way down *Tobacco Road.* Riding dangerously on his blue ox, called Babe, *Paul Bunyon* carved out the White Cliffs of Dover. Also *Little Bo Peep* softly crooned Home Sweet Home to her little lost sheep. Frankie murdered Johnnie in *Cold Blood,* with the weapon of Pistol Packing Mama.

Tarzan and Jane lived happily ever after *Swinging on a Star*, while Cheetah did the Hokey Pokey. *Romeo and Juliet* succumbed and went down as a twosome for *Whom the Bells Tolls.*

Ichabod Crane swept through Sleepy Hollow on the *Old Gray Mare*, who ain't what she used to be. Simple Simon ate the pie that was made for the king. Although, I don't understand why, for it was swarming with four and twenty blackbirds.

Heidi could look out her mountain top hideaway and see *Twinkle Twinkle Little Star. Snow White and the Seven Dwarfs* found *Paradise Lost* until the wicked stepmother stole it from under their nose with a bad apple. *Sleeping Beauty* awoke after *A Thousand and One Nights* to see the face of the Prince of Arabia. *The Owl and the Pussycat* serenaded each other under the light of the moon, while *Froggy Went A'Courting.*

Starlight, Starbright, kissed the little dipper. Jack climbed the bean stalk and floated on top of the Milky Way as he proclaimed what a big boy am I. *Peter Pan* and *Mother Goose* sailed away together to Never-Never Land, where dreams come true. Everyone knows *Fantasy Island* was patterned after Never-Never Land. At this point, I have to sneak in *My Blue Heaven* where dreams really do come true.

Brer Rabbit had a lingering attachment with Tar Baby. Brer Rabbit began to doubt he was a rabbit, perhaps he came from the descendants of *Roots. Little Big Horn* started *War and Peace.* The Genie made Aladdin's wish come true on a magic carpet through the *Arabian Nights.*

Mother Hubbard was so poor she couldn't feed *Lassie*, so she gave her away. But, *Lassie Come Home. Pocahontas*, in her wildest dreams could not believe *Our Town* would carry her namesake. *Mary Had a Little Lamb* that was well fed on *Green Grass of Wyoming.* Tiny Tim was the offspring of *Tom Thumb* and his sister was *Thumbelina.* When Clementine sank under the foaming brine, she heard the complaining voice of *The Ugly Duckling.*

Who's Afraid of Virginia Wolf dressed in sheep's clothing? Why, *Little Red Riding Hood,* of course. The cat and the fiddle played the *Fiddler on the Roof*, while Rome burned.

Chicken Little fell in love with Cockle Doodle Do way down on the farm. *Little Women* helped to take care of all the many children that lived with the homeless *Old Woman That Lived in a Shoe*. *Old King Cole* put on his foot gear and smothered *Puss-n-Boots*. The cat on the hot tin roof will have a *Hot Time in the Old Town Tonight*.

Tom Sawyer and his pal Jim floated down Old Man River and dwelt in *The House That Jack Built*. When Jack fell down and broke his crown, Jill ran screaming to fetch *Whistler's Mother*. *Wagon Train* disappeared and has *Gone With the Wind*. Rhett Butler's famous lament, "Frankly my dear, I don't give a damn," became Scarlett O'Hara's theme song.

The Little Engine who decided it could, puffed its way to the peak of *Old Smokey*. *She'll Be Coming Round the Mountain* when she comes, her and *The Farmer in the Dell* will feast on chicken and dumplings.

The sly old fox was always lurking around *Old MacDonald's Farm*. He never missed a meal. On Monday, he ate the *Little Red Hen*, on Tuesday; he had a little trouble, for he had to chase gobble, gobble here, gobble, goobie there, and everywhere before he caught him. On Wednesday, it was his day to go *To Market, To Market*, where he bought a fat pig. On Thursday, he ate a succulent meal called *The Little Lamb That Was*. On Friday, the menu called for Goosey, Goosey Gander, while Saturday was quack, quack entrée. On Sunday, he enjoyed his favorite moo-moo dessert. (So much for the sly old fox, that wound up with the slogan, Smart as a fox.)

Superman took Robin along and they flew over the cuckoo's nest to rescue a damsel in distress. Scrooge had a change of heart and gave from his abundance for *T'was the Night Before Christmas*. *Robin Hood* escaped the clutches of the Sheriff of Nottingham by hiding in Sherwood Forest where it was safe to court *My Fair Lady*.

May I Sleep in Your Barn Tonight Mister? Stormy Weather. Wouldn't it be a miracle to see three bobtail blind mice chasing the farmer's wife and playing I Spy? *Hickory Dickory Dock*, the mouse ran up and down Grandfather's clock. When the clock struck one, it struck no more, and the old man died from dead works.

Eeny, meeny, minie, moe, catch a pig by the toe and no one will have to pay to hear Babe squeal. Jack Spratt could eat no fat, his wife could eat no lean, so they ate crow. *Little Black Sambo* wound up *Naked Came I. Three Little Kittens* lost their mittens; their Mama said they could have no pie. They ran away and lapped up *Little Jack Horner*'s Christmas pie.

Long John Silver explored *Treasure Island* and discovered a rich *Bonanza. The Man in the Moon* viewed his image in *The Looking Glass* and saw the face of *The Man Who Launched a Thousand Ships.*

Dirty Harry washed his feet in a frying pan, and brushed his teeth with *Rawhide. The Hiding Place* was a refuge for *The Fugitive.* There seems to be no stopping place for fairy tales or the classics. One could go to the end of the rainbow.

So, I'll end this little sequel with a true tale about the death of the *Outlaw*, whose epithet was written in *Tombstone* and Ma Barker received *A Letter Edged in Black.*

I hope you got a chuckle or two out of the pages of the *Pathfinder*, for Wynkin, Blynkin, Nod and I are packed and ready to go on a *Sentimental Journey* to *London Derry,* flying on the continental express to see the Eiffel Tower, Big Ben and the place where London Bridge had fallen down.

Signed: The Mad Hatter.

My Dearest Daughter

Looking up your address, I decided to give you an update on a day with Mama. Thoughts of your dad are always uppermost in my mind. I realized there is no way to go but up. I woke up this morning, just as the sun was coming up. I rolled over and rubbed my sleepy eyes that seem to be a little stuck up. I sat up, slung my legs over the edge of the bed. I stood upright on legs that almost folded up. I straightened up my torn up bed. Tried to draw up a little bit of fresh air, for I seem to have caught a bit of a cold. I picked up my eye glasses, put them on, where they rested on my stopped up nose. I remembered to smile up at my pinup, a picture of a young soldier boy of World War II. Behind that smile was a look of sadness for at that time he was uprooted from a wife and family. That same guy and I were joined up in Holy Matrimony for forty-seven years. In 1991, he was taken up on the wings of a dove, riding on a heavenly updraft. Thinking of him caused me to tear up. Quivering lips and tears flowing, messed up the pretty lines and wrinkles in my face. Hanging up on a nearby wall were pictures of our five lovely children, who we both raised up to become adults.

They in turn brought up children for Grandma and Grandpa to cuddle up. Locking up the memories of my sweetheart, I walked up the hall to my blue and white updated kitchen, where I brewed up a cup of hot chocolate, opened up a can of biscuits, cooked up a plate of bacon and eggs. Cut up my eggs with a beat up fork and buttered up a tasty biscuit, ate up my good breakfast, drank up a cup of hot chocolate. My food and hot chocolate pepped me up. I washed up the dishes, cleaned up the kitchen. I picked up and shined up my living room. My adrenaline juices flowing, I turned up the volume on my radio, did a few sit ups and pushups while listening to upbeat music. Working up a sweat, I hit the shower, turned up the hot and cold water, stepped up into the bathtub and washed up. Cool, calm and collected, I perfumed up, powdered up and dressed up in my best get up.

I grabbed up my purse and the car keys, drove up town to Price Chopper, where I strolled up the aisles, all the while picking up and filling up a cart of groceries. I paid up at the cash register. Locked up my car, and drove up to my front door.

Snatching up two big bags, I wobbled up my front steps into the house and didn't stop until I reached the kitchen where I put up my groceries in the refrigerator and all the miscellaneous items I stacked up on a shelf. I went outside to do a little yard work. I burned up and burned out, my strength used up. I went back inside the house, where I sat down, put up my feet, deciding it was time to rest up a bit.

Somewhat later, getting a little hungry, I cooked up a cheeseburger smeared with catsup. I followed up my cheeseburger with a slice of upside down cake and washed it all down with a glass of Seven-Up. I called up my two delinquent cats, Buttercup and Cuddleup. I warmed up a can of Pet Milk, poured it up in their bowl that they quickly lapped up. Milk on their whiskers they licked up. Filled up and cleaned up, they sashayed across the floor to the living room where they jumped up on the couch. Cuddleup curled up and Buttercup lay down on his back, belly up and went to sleep.

At ten o'clock, I turned up the volume on the TV to catch up on the news. El Nino was kicking up a storm, tearing up towns and countryside's, uprooting trees and destroying homes. Road blocks were being set up to catch fleeing criminals and President Clinton vetoed the up coming budget. Fed up with all the bad news, the day's activities began to catch up with my seventy-two-year old used up body as sleep began to shut up my mind. In and out of sleep, I woke up confused and mixed up, my mind still plagued with the up mania. I groped for the up button on the TV. By the time I realized it had no up button, I knew the only place I was going was down. Finally, discovering the off button, I punched the right one, and staggered up the hall to my bedroom. I picked up my nightgown, barely getting it up over my head, where I all but fell up into the bed, between two clean, cool inviting sheets, right side up.

Soaring up into a state of euphoria lying flat on my back, I looked up and whispered a prayer of thanksgiving to the Heavenly Father up above. "Thank you, Lord, that I was able to stand upright on two feet this day, and for my lovely upstanding family and friends, my home, my health and Lord, if this should be my last sleep this night, take me up. My heart's desire is to be caught up, carried up and everything wrapped up when the roll is called up yonder. Uplifting thoughts of Heaven and love unfeigned forever, closed up my eyes and consciousness drifted up and away as the cats rose up to play.

P. S. Outside of everything, I'm doing fine. In the upcoming months, I'm planning on driving up to see you. As the old saying goes, a bad apple always turns up. Just wanted you to know health wise, I'm still on the up and up. Love and warmed up kisses. Mama.

Euple, Regina, Stephanie and Rhonda
Me and My Girls

Snowstorm

Saturday morning, January 3, 1989, the first snow of the season began to fall, dumping nine and a half inches of the white stuff in Randolph County and surrounding counties in Arkansas. By four p.m., workers and late shoppers trying to drive home in the blizzard began to panic; there was chaos along the highways as cars slid into the ditches or stalled on the steep hills.

Inside my home in the Washington Community, four miles southeast of Maynard, I was fascinated by the scene spread out before me, as I gazed out my window into a winter storm rapidly cascading down from above and covering everything in its path. The scene was unfolding like a picture postcard come to life, leaving the landscape clothed in a spotless white blanket of beauty. I decided to write the "Snowstorm" as I saw it. Yet the mystery of the snowflakes is forever sealed in heaven, and no human mind can ever do it justice, nor can the human hand ever duplicate it.

The Master Artist surely knew the countryside was His favorite canvas, for no where else is the picture as complete as it is in the country. And no other place shows such a display of beauty and grandeur as snow falling on the trees and open fields of the countryside.

Sunday morning the only splash of color in a white world was a red bird here and there and an occasional blue jay scampering up and down a tree trunk, along with several small snow birds chattering angrily at the injustice of the snow covered ground, for there was no place to set their cold naked feet, and not a morsel of food could be found.

The trees, standing still and silent were waiting expectantly for the finery made of pure white lace they were adorned with, covering their already heavy limbs. I was reminded of the trees of righteousness mentioned in Isaiah 61. As I beheld their elegant white garments festooned with diamonds, I thought surely these are "Trees of Righteousness." Every bush and shrub was bowing low in obedience to the Master Painter. A lone pine tree stood in the middle of an open field, drooping sadly toward the ground, holding its heavy weight of beauty. The snow birds were flitting in and out of its sheltering arms. Underneath its

135

branches they found a haven of safety. The fence posts were wearing crowns of crystal as they supported the heavily laden fence, garnished with strands of white pearls. The power lines were wearing a huge garland of splendor (as big as a man's arm), from post to post, hill to hill. The weight they held was so great; lines broke all over the county, causing many homes to be out of electricity for several hours. In all the years my family and I have lived here and had electricity, I have never seen the power lines holding this much weight.

The mysteries and glory of God could be seen as far as the eye could see. How small and insignificant is man and his environment in the face of the "Great Creator of the Universe."

The silence was so profound; I stood in awe of its magnificence. Animals were holed up in their winter homes snug and warm. The car, sitting in the drive, looked like a huge white bug from outer space, with two large eyes peering out from under its shell, staring in the direction of our home and getting ready to pounce on the strange white building that was wearing a mantle of perfection and beauty.

Even the old barn roof was wearing the same beauty. The cleats on the electric poles were covered in white, giving one the impression of some giant creature wearing a brown suit, festooned with large white buttons, from its neck to its feet. The road was a shining white ribbon, stretching out into a panoramic view of loveliness, without a track to mar its beauty.

The dictionary describes snow as frozen water in the form of soft, white flakes. Randolph County received a lot of frozen water in the feathery stuff all day Saturday—a Godsend to the farming lands.

The above story was first published in The Star Herald *in 1989. The Storyteller in 2007.*

The snowstorm of 1989

Me, a Stranger

Rhonda (Riney) Byrd

Upon a dark sea, I traveled, so weary and so sad,
For life to me had brought no gladness, nor had
It gave me wealth, or fame, no riches to call my own.
I sought for the things of life around the world, alone.
I trod where famous people had trod, a Stranger.
I sang the same sweet songs, the angels before me had sung,
I walked with a heavy heart, of one who seems as the dead,
But even then, no one seemed to care.

Life holds sorrows, always looking, looking, but never finding,
Things the heart does crave, nor finding peace,
Along the dreary roads of life I traveled, alone and unwanted.

I longed for peace of a broken heart, but peace came not.
I dreamed dreams of paradise, but found it not;
Only a broken dream along with a broken heart.
I feared the eyes of mortals, always prying, prying,
Me, a Stranger.

I sought for the things of the world, not love or eternal life;
I swam the salty oceans; I lay on the pearly white sands of time,
I danced in the moonlight, and sang to the stars;
I looked, ever looked for some beckoning hand,
And when things of the world did fail me, I turned then to
    mankind
And again I faced the bitter tears of failure, for men are
Only one more thing of the world, and seeth not the little
Things like me, a Stranger.

I walked in a garden of peace one day, I heard a still small voice
And it said to me, Me!! a Stranger,
"Come unto me, ye that are heavy laden, and I will give you
    rest."
And now my wondering life is past, a marvelous peace I've
    found
At last; Me, Just a stranger.

138

The Old Log Barn

We built our old log barn in the early fifties to house our many animals we had acquired. It stood the test of time and become more than just a barn. With all the syringes and needles, the master kept, it became a veterinarian's office. Many babies were born in its interior; many of them on a cold winter night. A preemie was often taken to the house where it was nursed to health. We rejoiced at a new birth it held in its embrace, but were sad when death stalked its portals.

It held sweet hay and grain (never let it be said the farmer's animals ever went hungry). It was a shelter from a rainstorm when the family got caught too far from the house.

It was a business adventure for several years. Equipped with a big cream separator that poured out rich gold that fifteen or twenty Holsteins and Jersey cows produced. Holsteins for their milk and Jerseys for their butterfat. Dipping into that big can of cream and whipping it up to go on a piece of pie was a heavenly dish. (A big refrigerator kept that can of gold, sweet and fresh.) We got a check once a week for that can of sweet cream from a creamery in Missouri and Illinois. It was no small feat filling up those cans, for we milked the herd of cows twice a day by hand. The separated milk with all the butterfat taken out of it was no good for anything but the pigs and the many cats that roamed inside. (We sure had some fat cats and pigs.) To them it was like slurping a huge foamy, yummy milkshake.

The old barn was a refuge for birds and the many chickens that used it for a scratch pad and rolled in its dirt floor. The old barn was a playground for three children. Cowboy skills were practiced around outside walls as it became a rodeo arena. Davy Crockett and Daniel Boone often visited its compound from time to time, wearing a homespun suit, a coonskin cap and moccasins, carrying long guns. Indians were their enemy as the Riney Fort was raided by dozens of redskins on any given day. "Could that be a couple of Indian scalps hanging from Daniel Boone's belt?" The old barn had many scars where bullets and arrowheads had penetrated from the many battles that were fought in and around it.

Nails were hammered into its logs where a castoff shirt or cap was hung, long enough for a bird to make a nest in its folds. It was often a ship at sea with the chief captain and his small crew. It became a lot of far away places of grander, its logs faded into marble walls and shiny floors where kings and queens resided. It became a big cathedral with all its glitter and glamour, packed with a vast audience. The little boy who grew up to be a minister delivered a stirring message. With a funny sense of humor, two little boys became clowns, smeared with mama's stolen make-up.

Yes, the old barn was all things to its family. Like a grand old lady, who after many years began to show her age, her doors began to sag and the rain began to pour inside. Folding up its logs after many years of service, it gave up the ghost. A big new barn with a hall down its middle took the old barn's place under the expertise of The Farmer.

The old barn—a relic of the past had laughter and beauty the new barn never had for it will always live in the hearts of the family who grew up and grew older under its tin roof and walked its dirt floor.

The new barn never heard any children at play, nor saw two special men (my Dad and husband) and two strong mules at work. Yes, the old barn stood the test of time with dignity and honor, holding memories of freedom and contentment that will never die.

Jamie's cat playing hide and seek among
the hay in the old log barn

The Necklace

The first time she saw it, it was lying on a bed of gauze while it blinked its magic and loveliness up at her. The pervading atmosphere was cloaked with excitement that wove itself around her rapidly beating heart as she whispered, "Jasper."

A twenty-three-year-old soldier vacationing in Holland in 1945 purchased that pretty jewel to send to his true love across the sea. He would love to see her eyes light up when it arrived.

No, Jasper was beyond the means of a common soldier boy, but the one she held in her hands was wrapped with love. It spoke of a million dollar's worth of dreams tied up with caresses and untouchable moon beams.

A work of art it was. Hanging from a black cord was a lavender rose, surrounded by pink rose buds. Pale green, blue and white tear drops placed here and there with magenta colored leaves set among the rest with a tassel of tiny multicolored beads at the bottom.

She was only nineteen-years-old. Ah, he thought SHE was a work of art. She was small and petite, long black tresses that resembled black diamonds, with eyes of brown that captured his heart right from the start.

The necklace lay like a beacon up on her breast for all the world to see. She wore it proudly as any piece of expensive pearls of nobility that ever graced the neck of a queen.

In 1998, fifty three years later, she still wears it proudly as she feels his love reaching out to her beyond the grave. An inexpensive, small pendant worth more to her than silver or gold.

My husband, my love, sent it to me in a little box, stamped with "Magic and Stardust," from across the rolling sea.

The Itch

Back in the 1930's, before modern medicine came along, the "Itch" was a common disorder among school children. Mostly in the wintertime. It could be caught on contact with anyone who had it. Children were always holding hands or touching each other. It generally hung on most of the winter, so it was called "The Seven Year Itch." The only remedy that was available back then was a vile smelling concoction called sulphur and grease. It was smeared all over the body, arms, legs and in between the fingers and toes. Little tiny blisters formed and often became irritated that made open wounds and that's where it itched the worse. I think the smell of that sulphur penetrated the inner core of the body—even the walls of our house were saturated with the smell.

Every night before bedtime, my sister and I played a game of smear and smell, smear and smell. She'd smear that nasty stuff all over my naked body and I'd smell. Without it, the itching was terrible! No matter how much you bathed, the smell lingered all the next day, then it was time to do it all over again.

Setting or standing by a wood burning stove would bring out the scent even stronger than ever. Most of the children reeked of it anyway, something everyone accepted. It was a way of life back then.

I don't know which was the worse, the itching or that foul smelling ointment that never completely went away until spring. Then the house and all our clothes and bedding were fumigated with gallons of boiling water and lye soap.

Even today, when the breeze is coming from a certain direction—I get a whiff of a strange odor, reminding me of that nasty yellow salve called Sulphur and Grease. One not only itched day and night, one smelled to high heaven as well.

Being one of those little girls of the '30's, I scratched and clawed my way up the ladder of success. (My ace in the hole was wearing golden scented cosmetics—Knock 'em dead.)

Elizabeth Arden never had it so good with her millions of dollars worth of make-up. Her magic only spread so far, where as our make-up left a golden sheen applied to the whole body that improved ones looks and worked miracles.

Head lice was also a scrounge of many of the bigger schools. Somehow, I escaped that affliction in our small country school. My sister, a clean freak, the housekeeper and house mother of our home would have had a conniption fit if I had brought head lice to our house. The only way anyone could get rid of them was by combing the hair with a fine tooth comb over and over. Sis would have pulled me bald-headed by wearing out a dozen combs or more. If that didn't get rid of them, she would have used a razor on my head. Bald was certainly not the in thing in 1930. Shaved heads of today would have been the laughing stock of the country. We never heard those three words—"Bald is beautiful," nor would it have met with our approval. In our lingo, we would have reversed that by saying, "Bald is ugly."

Horror of horrors if such would have been my fate had my sister stooped to that level. Knowing my big Sis, she probably wouldn't have been satisfied even with my shaved head. She wouldn't have stopped until she gave my naked pate a vigorous scrubbing of kerosene. (According to my Dad, kerosene was the miracle cure for almost anything.)

Although my sister loved me dearly, I often wondered if maybe she wouldn't have been a little devious and thought about lighting a match to my kerosene covered head if the kerosene itself didn't work. Knowing her as I did, I know she would not have been satisfied until she stuck me in a tub full of blistering hot water and scrubbed me raw from head to toe.

The "Itch" was bad enough, no telling what would have happened to me with head lice. I probably wouldn't have any hair at all today, for she would have gone the last mile of the way with all of those concoctions she could think of.

Head lice, in my sister's book, was a disgrace—big time.

Possum Pearl the Boxer Puppy

Stephanie (Riney) Tidwell

This story is dedicated to Paxton Marshal Dillion— (nicknamed Possum Pearl), a boxer puppy that grew up in a house filled with love. In other words—she was a spoiled, but lovable dog! Sadly, she left us all in 2007

Hello! My name is Possum Pearl. I am a little girl. I'm not sure what Boxer puppy means, but that's what I heard my mommy tell her friend that's what I am. My fur is a soft brown, my toes have white tips and I have a white upside down heart on my chest and a black muzzle. My tail is just a stub, but my ears are long. My mommy says making them short is not nice to do to puppies.

I am a member of a very nice family that loves me and I love them. There's my mommy, Uncle David, and Bubbie and Grandma Riney. Mommy says Bubbie is my big brother, but I don't think we look anything alike. We live in the country on a hill with a pond on one side and a creek on the other.

We have two cats, one is named Kit-Kat and the other is Smokey. And we also have a horse named Chief (*Chief passed away in 2006)*. I chase him and he kicks at me. Mommy says that's just one of my shenanigans. I'm always digging, wading in the pond or the creek, or just running in the fields. I love the country! Running free with the wind in my face.

There are so many things to smell here. Its spring right now and the flowers are blooming, the birds are singing. Birds? Singing? Oh yes! That reminds me. Those birds have been in the yard way too long. It's time to chase them off. Oh yes, chase them off! This is my territory. Mommy! Mommy! Let me out. I have to do something really important.

Whine, whine! Ohhh! She's getting up. I can hardly wait. Hurry, Mommy, hurry. Maybe if I jump around a little, she will hurry faster. Yes! The door's opening. I'm out! I'm out! There those birds are. Run! Run faster. There they go. They are flying away. How do they do that? They get so high in the air and out of my reach. Maybe next time if I run even faster, I can catch one. Yes, next time, run faster. That's what I'll do.

I guess I had better go potty while I'm outside. Hey! There's something moving over in the tall grass. What is it? I'll just sneak up on it slowly and crouch down real low. It will never see me pounce. Oh, rats! It's just Kit-Kat.

Oh, no! Get away! Quit rubbing all over me! Your fur gets up my nose and makes me sneeze. Ach-choo! Ach-choo! See?

Now hurry! Let's go down to the pond and see what we can find before Mommy calls me to come back inside. Come on! You're lagging behind. Run a little. There's a fish splashing in the pond. Yes, yes, there's another one! Look! There's a dragonfly. Kit-Kat get it. Jump, Kit-Kat, jump! You missed it. That's okay, I'll get him. He's flying low. I think I can just about reach him, just a little more.

Oh, no! Silly dragonfly! Look what you made me do. I got my feet all wet and muddy. Now, my mommy will have to wipe my feet off with a towel before I can go inside. She doesn't like her floors dirty. Maybe if I roll around in the grass they will dry faster. Oh! This feels so good. Sunshine on my tummy, a nice breeze blowing. I think I'll just lie here all day.

What? What was that? I think I hear my mommy calling. I'll see you later Kit-Kat. I'm coming! There's my mommy at the door. Whoops! She sees my wet and muddy feet. Oh, thank goodness. It's okay. She's smiling and patting my head.

Sorry, Mommy. It was an accident, it really was. You see, there was this dragonfly...what? Oh. She wants me to raise my paws one at a time so she can clean them off.

She's putting her arms around me. Ohhhh! This is the best part of all. She's giving me a big hug and a bigger kiss on the muzzle. It makes me all tickly and tingly inside. I love my mommy.

I think I'll go take a nap by the window now. Bye.

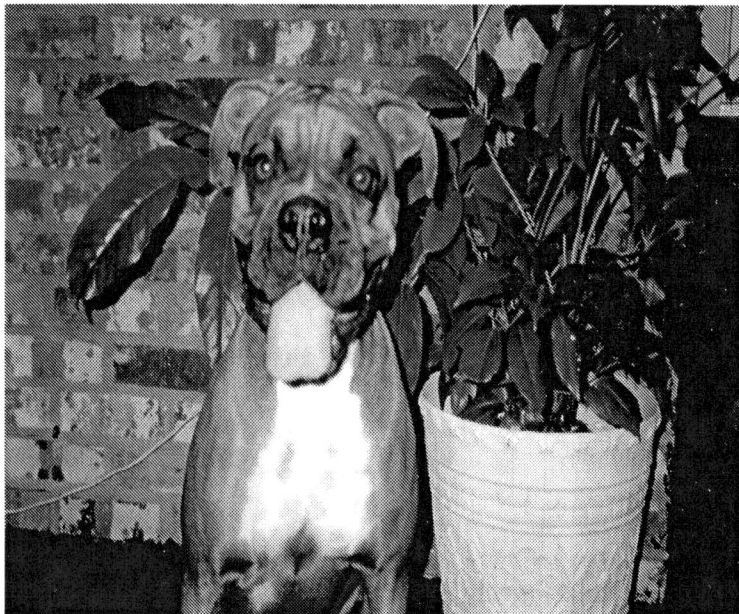

Paxton Marshall Dillion 3/15/1996-3/6/2007

Sticks and Stones and a Fisherman's Dream

What does sticks and stones and a fisherman's dream have in common, you ask? Being from the old school of pencil and paper, I'll take my pencil in hand and enlighten your mind as I proceed to tell you my daddy's story of sticks and stones and a fisherman's dream.

If Daddy had access to my version of his story today, he would probably give me that little crooked grin of his and tell me, "That's a pretty damn good story, Sis. You told it like it was. But to say the least, I was a little surprised at the unusual twist it took at the end."

Daddy disliked anything that made a constant, continual noise, such as mockingbirds, blue jays, guinea hens, turkey gobblers, crowing roosters, and whippoorwills. He always kept a hand-made sling-shot dangling from his hip pocket for the mockingbirds and blue jays. That crude weapon he made himself out of a small forked tree limb with two strips of inner tube from a worn out automobile tire and a leather pouch attached to hold his rocks. Those rocks were like bullets in Daddy's hands, for he was a pro carrying a mean-looking forked stick. He'd let fly at his target, his eyes flashing fire and brimstone, with the intention of doing bodily harm. Seven times out of ten he always got his bird.

As for the guinea hens, turkey gobblers, crowing roosters and whippoorwills, he always kept a supply of rocks handy or pick up a broken limb that had fallen. With feet racing and wings flapping, they would scurry off behind the barn, or head for the woods. They surely had Daddy's number when the sticks and rocks began to fly, as he would say, "Them dad-burn critters ain't nothing but a blasted nuisance. I wish I never had to hear another one as long as I live." He meant every word of it too.

Ah, the whippoorwills, they were his worst enemy, for they came out at night and disturbed his sleep. Daddy, with his long-handle underwear or a night shirt on, would wake up the rest of the household by trooping outside—slamming doors and yelling fiery epitaphs—all hours of the night. Armed with more sticks and stones, he aimed them as best he could in their direction in the darkness. With all the commotion he made, silence would rein over the countryside for awhile. But an hour or so later, they would be back, serenading him again.

Danged if the air around Daddy's bed wasn't blue. Great balls of fire. When riled, Daddy could spit out a few choice words that could curl the whippoorwill's feathers. "You son-to-bitches, get the hell out of here. I'd like to get some sleep sometime tonight."

Satisfied they had left to other territory, he'd storm back inside to bed, mouthing his complaint all the while before falling asleep from exhaustion. Poor Daddy, with his hang ups and frustration with all the racket, was quite a man in more ways that one.

As a dad, he was the best. Yet the rest of the family could not understand his dilemma, for we all slept like babies, lulled to sleep by the song of the whippoorwills.

Thirty-eight years after his death, when I hear a whippoorwill call in the early morning hours, I'm often reminded of Daddy's voice sending an echo out over the hills and hollows of Arkansas, while the rest of the world was asleep. (Except the family, of course.) I smile in remembrance and wipe a melancholy tear away.

On the other hand, Daddy loved to fish. He could set on a river or pond bank all day long (but his favorite spot was a shady, tree-lined river bank), holding a cane pole, his hook baited with a wiggly worm. (He kept dozens of them in a can at his feet.) The day before he had dug up worms from around the barn, or else he picked horse flies off of a dozen lounging cows on the farm. No fancy rod and reel from the store for him, for he liked the feel of a sturdy cane pole he'd cut and dried himself, by golly!

At those fun-filled moments of his life, time ceased to exist, for he was living high on the crest of the river of contentment and relaxation. He had the patience of Job and even the birds could not disturb his little paradise. Excitement riding high, and an eight hour day ahead of him, he was at peace with the world at large. Fishing was a little bit of Heaven on earth. Pure mitigated pleasure was pulling one fish after another into his possession. All day long.

Setting in the shade of a tree on a hot summer day with the sweat pouring down his face, dripping off his nose and chin and soaking his shirt, did not stop him. I don't think he was even aware of the heat he was so involved with what he was doing, playing a fisherman's symphony. He'd wipe the sweat away with a smelly sweat stained handkerchief he carried in his pocket for just such an emergency for he knew he would need it up in the heat of the day. After wiping sweat and a runny nose, he'd wave that ole pole over that watery span with a flourish of pride, while talking to all the fish.

"Come on, ole fish, take a bite of this big juicy worm I have for you. You know it has your name on it."

Relaxing against a tree in total comfort, he would spy a huge old catfish playing around in the shallows. With a gleam in his eye, he would rear back and boast, "Ole catfish, you will be mine before this day is over."

Sure enough, more than likely he would catch it. He would jump to his feet, doing the St. Vitas Dance, happy lingo rolling off his tongue as he proclaimed, "Whoppee! Hot damn, I got him."

Admiring his catch with a happy smile, he would say, "Look at you, ain't you a dad-burn beauty?" Drooling over its size, he would smack his lips with relish. "By cracky (his favorite saying), I'm gonna have you for supper tonight. M-m-m-m, I can pert neart taste you already."

He loved to eat them almost as much as he did catching them. Nothing was any better than a plate of golden fried fish, served up with a delicious hunk of cornbread and a cold glass of milk.

He'd string that catfish on a strong, sturdy cord staked out at the water's edge, where he could keep a watchful eye on his mouth-watering supper. Then he would throw another baited hook into that beautiful tree-lined spot for the umpteenth time, basking in his luck. Ah, yes, there was no other place in the world as beautiful on a bright spring or summer day for Daddy. Happiness was a free flowing river at his feet, like an over-flowing, bubbling fountain, spilling out all over him with pleasure and delight. He was a kid again, playing his favorite game. Only one word would describe his day—SUPER!

Returning home just before sundown with a long string of bass, crappy, and a big old catfish or two, dangling from his hand, he wore a contented, satisfied smile of achievement, whistling a merry tune, for by nature, Daddy was a whistler.

I can see him now, tripping down our dusty gravel road, wearing a floppy straw hat, a checkered shirt, his overall legs rolled up halfway to his knees. His shoes were sopping wet, for he had slipped into the water at least twice, tussling with a fighter and smelling like fish and dried sweat. Oh, well, what the heck. Working men always sweat. Norman Rockwell, a famous artist of the early 1900's, must have had Daddy in mind when he painted the "Fishing Boy." For he, too, was whistling, wearing a straw hat, overalls rolled up, with his shoes laced together and hanging around his neck. He carried a cane pole and a brace of fish with a small dog following along behind. Daddy was somewhat older than the "Fishing Boy," but he was a kid at heart.

Happy Fishing, Daddy.

I never caught the fishing fever from my daddy. For one thing, when I was small, I couldn't be still long enough, when I got older, I had other fish to fry.

In 2002, my family and I—my two daughters and their mates, along with three grandchildren, were vacationing in Florida. The boys were having so much fun fishing in the ocean; I decided I'd try my luck. As a greenhorn, I attempted to sling that rod out over that mighty span, with a lot of near misses, until I kinda got the hang of it. I guess it was beginners luck—I began to feel a tug on that line and right away I caught one fish after another. Several were small sharks. Suddenly, I felt a tremendous tug as something streaked across those rolling waves, almost bowling me over. I began to scream, "Tom, what do I do now? What do I do now?" as I ran along the beach with a death grip on that rod, all the time cranking like mad on that little do-ma-fitch-it on the side of the rod. This Grandma was having a conniption fit struggling with that huge critter. With Tom's help, I finally wrestled a huge stingray to shore. Talk about excitement! I think Daddy, the sneaky old devil, was standing behind me, tempting me to say, "Hot damn, I caught him!"

I think my family had more fun watching me than they did fishing. After seventy some years, I understood Daddy's excitement, and love of fishing. How I wished he could have been there. He would have been at the highest peak of his life fishing on that huge body of water, "By cracky!"

Tom said he taught me how to fish, his next project was to teach me to cuss and drink.

Dedicated to all the fishermen, especially to my son-in-law, Tom, who also loves to fish and cuss!

Herman Tutt

The Letter and the Lunchbox

Rhonda (Riney) Byrd

I remember when I was little, one of the highlights of the day was when Daddy came home from his job at Sallee's Handle Mill. Everyday we would listen for the sound of the truck coming up the hill. One of us would yell, "Daddy's home!" and then the four of us, Mick, Dick, Regina and me would run out to meet him and welcome him home. He almost always had a smile on his face, happy to see his kids that he was so proud of.

Dad carried a black metal lunch box that Mom packed everyday with bologna sandwiches wrapped up in waxed paper, left over biscuits from breakfast or other leftovers from the night before. The best part of his lunches was Mom's fried pies. Sometime there were fruit pies, but what we all loved more than any other were Mom's fried chocolate pies.

I think about Dad, setting down to lunch and seeing a fried chocolate pie and the sacrifice he must have made, because he always left a portion of his delicious pie for us to find when he came home. One of us would take the lunch box to the kitchen and go through its contents. If there was a small piece of chocolate pie, we were in heaven.

Once inside, Mom and Dad would settle on the couch, smooching a little, and telling each other what had happened during the day. We all got a turn to talk while in the background the radio played country music. Dad might tell us how he had played a practical joke on one of his co-workers. The boys and Dad would usually wind up on the floor, wrestling, until someone got hurt.

Dad worked hard at the mill, and came home to work the farm. There were cows, horses, pigs, and sheep to feed, hay to mow and take up, crops to put in and harvest. There were fences to mend, and wood to cut for the old wood stove that sat in the living room.

Later in the evening, long after dark and after chores were done and supper was over, Dad would take his Bible and sit in "his" chair, open up his book that contained all he needed to know about living a good and pleasing life. After reading a few passages, he would fall asleep and Mom would call that he needed to come to bed. The next day, he did it all over again.

God was first in Dad's life, his wife and children came second, that's what the book told him and he tried to follow God's rules and obey Him in everyway. Dad fully expected his children to follow and obey his rules.

Sometimes Dad's rules and expectations seemed harsh and unreasonable. We would often go to Mom to run interference. More often than we liked, she would agree with Dad and we knew we couldn't budge that united front. At times, Mom too, felt Dad might be a little too steadfast and she would try talking to him, try to get him to see a different point of view. Dad could be a little stubborn and Mom would resort to the power of the pen.

Mom would sit down and put her thoughts on paper and carefully fold the note and place it in the lunch box for him to read on his lunch break. Occasionally, Dad would relent and we were allowed to have our way. Just as often, though, he was firm and even Mom knew to give up.

When I was a teenager, about fifteen-years-old and a freshman in high school, I developed a crush on an "older man." He had graduated high school a couple of years before. For some reason, he started hanging out at a small café across the road from the school building and he would talk to the girls.

When he started driving by our house in the evening, Dad got wind of what was going on. One afternoon after school, I had ridden the horse down the road and had topped the next hill, when "he" drove by and stopped to talk. Dad saw us and as clear as a bell, I heard him holler, "Rhonda Lynn, git on home, now!"

After that incident, Dad tried to talk to me, but I was also stubborn and when "he" gave me his class ring, I accepted. Things got very tense at that time. In our little house, it was impossible to avoid each other, but that's what we tried to do.

Mom, as usual, did her best to make peace between us. She told Dad to let it go, this crush would pass. She said the more he made over it, the more he was pushing me toward "him."

I think Dad was afraid. He was new at this teenage girl rebellion and didn't know how to handle the situation. It broke my heart that my daddy was so angry with me, yet I couldn't let go either. This unhappy time went on for a few more weeks until Mom took pen in hand again.

That day, after school, I was in the kitchen by myself. As I recall no one else was in the house. I saw the lunch box on the table and even at that age, I couldn't resist the thought of a fried chocolate pie.

I opened the box and I saw the letter. It wasn't mine to read, but I was a nosy teen. Mom had poured her heart out to Dad on my behalf. She told him that I was a good girl and too young to decide on my future with anyone. If he would let go and give me some space, it wouldn't be long before I realized the crush for what it was.

Just as I finished reading the letter, Daddy suddenly appeared at the doorway. He knew I had read the letter and I knew he knew it. By this time, there were tears on both our cheeks and within seconds, Dad had crossed the room and his arms were around me, holding me tight and whispering, "I'm sorry." It was my turn to say, "I'm sorry, too."

My mom was so wise. I don't know how she pulled it off. How had she engineered Dad and me alone in the house that day when it was usually full of noisy kids? Did she know I would read the letter?

And she had been right. Before the week was out, I had given back the ring and my crush was over.

Every time I see a black metal lunchbox in an antique store or a magazine, I go back in my mind to our kitchen and I am reminded of my daddy and his love for me and all his children.

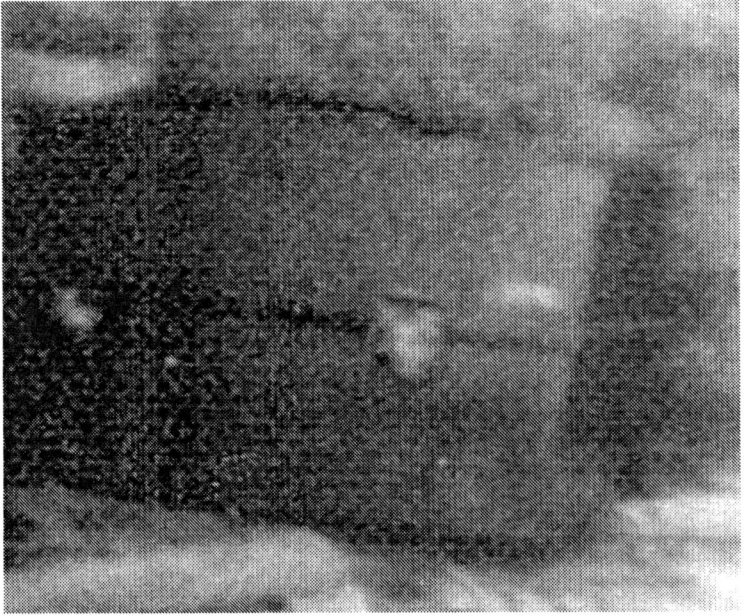

The Lunchbox

The Bedroom Suit

In the spring of 1946, World War II had been over for a year. My soldier boy came home to stay. We were embarking on a new way of life—as citizens of our community, as we prepared to move into our first home.

That little castle on the hill was a two room log cabin we rented, along with a few acres of land that was Joe's first endeavor to farm on his own. With a couple of big strong mules, a wagon and a plow, he was all set to make our first cotton crop.

The next step was filling up those two rooms with what furniture we could buy. I had acquired a wood cook stove, a table and four chairs, a kitchen cabinet, and a wardrobe. All we lacked was a bed.

After Pearl Harbor, many girls and their boyfriends rushed into marriage as the men were headed for the war-front. Joe and I among them. All the wives received an army pension, and I had a good-sized nest egg put away. I was determined to buy not only a bed, but a bedroom suit. Such a luxury I had never had. Shopping in a well-known furniture store in town, I spotted "The Bedroom Suit," and fell in love. Ah, the bed was a blonde maple, four poster affair, with a huge chest of drawers, and a large dresser with an oval mirror across its broad width, made up the three piece set. Talk about luxury. That bedroom suit was the epitome of wealth and I gloried in its beauty every time I lay down on its softness, or stored our clothes in all those roomy drawers. Looking into that lovely mirror was like watching a fairy tale as I heard the old familiar cry, "Mirror, mirror, on the wall, who is fairest of them all?"

All dressed up in my best bib and tucker, powered and perfumed, a night on the town with my man, I felt like I was the fairest of them all when he whispered softly in my ear, "You are beautiful, honey."

No other home has ever been as precious as that little house all gussied up with shiny new furniture, with homemade curtains at the windows. It was truly "Our home, sweet home."

We ordered a new battery operated radio from "Aldine's" that kept our little house jumping and jiggling every day. Sometime, he and I cut a figure eight all over those old wooden

156

floors and fell onto that pretty bed exhausted, like two children playing make believe.

To round out the year of 1946—in November, that little house became a nursery as our first born; a big strapping baby boy came along to brighten our little corner of the world.

Farming, cooking, cleaning, washing and taking care of a baby took up much of our time, yet Joe had time to hitch up the team to the wagon and make a trip to the grocery store four miles away. Or we would visit the in-laws every weekend, just for the sheer fun of rocking along on a country road.

Sad to say that pretty bed wore out and fell apart many years ago and was replaced with an antique iron bedstead. It, alongside the same dresser and chest holds a prominent place in my bedroom today, some sixty years later. The two pieces are a little worse for wear, a few scars and scratches adorn the finish. A few drawer pulls were lost along the way and some of the drawers stick at times, but all in all, they are still filling their purpose of holding clothes, underwear, socks and mementos of the past. Pictures of four generations have set upon its well-worn top. Brushes, combs, and make-up of three teenage daughters were scattered all over the dresser as they primped and powered in front of that jumbo mirror. Now and then it seems I catch a scent of shaving cream and hair tonic called Brill Cream from two teenage boys and their Dad.

In the early '50's and beyond, both dresser and chest held baby clothes, blankets, and diapers. They crooned a lullaby as they held tiny garments and pj's in their embrace. Later on, both boys and their three sisters, piled dresses, slips, shirts and jeans all over the chest. At times like that, they were reminded of the song Mama often sang, "When I Lay My Burdens Down."

Today the old mirror is showing its age as several bare spots show through, yet it has served the family well. It gloried in our youth, watched the family grow older, and brooded over its children. It silently applauded every achievement, and sagged at the seams at every disappointment. Perhaps it shed a few dry tears when the children left the nest. Memories haunt their countenance when they passed by its shining face, intent on mischief and mayhem. It seems I hear an echo of a chuckle as nothing escaped its all seeing mirrored face knowing the heart of a child.

As far as Mama, my mirror has never laughed at me, for we have gone back together from the first day we met, forming a lasting friendship as I caressed its beautiful contours with wonder and admiration. Even when I looked my worse, it always saw my best qualities as a wife and a mother. It always knew the next time I looked into its depths, I'd be all dolled up—my hair a shining halo, and with a touch of make-up on, a pretty dress rustling around my shapely legs, it whistled its approval and said, "What a pretty lady you are today." My spouse and the children all agreed. Even the chest looking down from its regal height seemed to nod its head in agreement.

Remembering all the babies, the joy and childish laughter, the years in between, I wipe a tear or two away and I'm reminded of the little ditty I used to sing to my children, "This little boy (or girl) of mine."

In 2005, the two pieces and their adopted bed look out over a pretty light green room with white lacy curtains at the windows, with a shiny white floor at their feet. A clothes closet, holding an elderly ladies clothes that once hung in a small wardrobe is a far cry from the young couple and the little cabin of the 1940's. In 1947, we moved into a three room house in the heart of the woods where our second little boy was born on February 18, in that same four poster bed, with no attending nurse or doctor.

As far as the bed, it's probably the oldest of the three. Iron bedsteads never die—in time they just rust away. It also holds decades of performances as it embraced our family with loving care and held a young couple securely for many years as it holds a grandmother's heart in its embrace today. It holds secrets it will never tell of dreams and aspirations whispered far into the night by two lovers. It cradled the two of us gently underneath its warm quilts and blankets as it sweetly lulled us to sleep for over half a century.

The man who stole my heart over sixty years ago died with a heart attack in 1991, leaving me to sleep in its comfortable resting place alone. Lying on those well-worn pillows, they soaked up a river of grieving, heart-broken tears. On awakening in the middle of the night, I wondered, where are you, my love?

Those times I emptied out my soul and cried again. In days of yore there was laughter and happiness, especially when the Mr. cuddled the Mrs. in his arms and whispered sweet nothings in her ears. Yet there were nights we turned our backs to each other after a quarrel. It not only cradled us in our youth, it watched my once jet black hair turn to white. It saw my unblemished skin marked with wrinkles and grooves of a grandmother past her prime. I can't get around so well anymore to polish its aging mirrored face. Yet my mirror and I don't care whether we make a good impression or not, we are too broken-down and worn out to care.

With all the modern day furniture I have these days in a much bigger house, these three pieces are my prized possessions, for I still see them through the eyes of a young bride and her handsome husband. Yesterday setting before my mirror, for a moment, I captured his reflection at my back, flashing me that little crooked smile he often wore when he was bent on doing mischief. Bending over my shoulder, he kissed me on the cheek and whispered, "You are beautiful, Mom."

Perhaps he is somewhere looking into the mirror of eternity, responding in a lover's voice to mirror, mirror on the wall, as he loudly proclaims, "Euple is the fairest of them all!"

The bedroom suit

Green Tea

Years ago when I was an obnoxious teenager, I thought my big sister said jump up and sit down. So I jumped up and she knocked me back down. What she really said was, "Am I gonna have to knock some sense into your fat head for I'm gonna jump all over you, directly. Just remember, I've got your number."

I figured my number was about up seeing that fire in her eyes with a knot on my head as big as a goose egg. She had the nerve to accuse me of whining like a baby! It sure was an eye-opener though as it made my feel bad hurt. So mad I couldn't see straight, I felt like I got the short end of the stick, so I told daddy on her. Looking her square in the eyes, he said, "There's more than one way to skin a cat. If you want the fur to fly, turn it loose in a briar patch." That was just his way of saying, "Lay off that child."

Sister thought Daddy was running off at the mouth for she wasn't having any of that bull. Giving me the evil eye, she stalked out of the house, practically foaming at the mouth. I got my revenge, however, when Daddy put his foot down. "Put her on bread and lick-um dab for two days. Made with milk was bad enough, but made with water was worse. Anyway you slice it; it sure didn't taste like sausage and biscuits. Lick-em dab was made with a little lard, flour and water and seasoned with a small ingredient called Iron Stomach. You had to have an iron stomach to eat it.

As we were eating a tasty breakfast, Sister glared at me with that, "you just wait," look. Oh, well, the cat's made short work out of the leftovers. Gravy of any kind was a cat's meow, so they say. Home is where the heart is, but Sister was about to run away from home. Mean as she was, I'd have run away with her.

Sister, pretty as a picture, especially in her glad rags, for the most part had the run of the house, ruling us with kid gloves. She allowed no sass from her kid sister still wet behind the ears. When I got testy, according to Sis, I was acting ugly. She threatened me with a dose of "Green Tea," (a peach tree switch to be exact).

Bitter as Epsom Salts was, I'd rather she would douse me with that nose holding mess than one of Green Tea. Somehow, I never developed a taste for Green Tea.

There were no flies on Sis. I never could pull the wool over her eyes. Eyes in the back of her head fit my Sister to a T. Seems like she was much worse when her nose was out of joint, then she would fly into me like a house afire with both fist doubled up. Snot and tears ran like a sugar tree and she had the gaul to tell me it was for my own good. I never could understand that baloney. Can you imagine any one giving an innocent child like I was that kind of treatment? For my own good was an understatement.

To get my revenge, I'd kick her cat or Fido the dog. That made her even hotter under the collar and I'd have to swallow some more Green Tea. The next day or two, it rained cats and dogs and I wondered if maybe the Big Man Upstairs wasn't giving me a dose of my own medicine, for the old house groaned with labor pains and the laying hens laid hard-boiled eggs.

We never did find out what the Watcha-ma-call-it was raining down the big river in the sky. Scared me so bad, I swore I would never kick the dog or cat ever again. I'd often heard the story of the cat's Aunt Jane, perhaps her and all her cats left their calling card.

Our mice had a case of catawompus which was often fatal. But in our case, the mice chased the cat, which ran up a tree. The mice played ring around the rosy with our lazy, good-for-nothing cat. Hearing old Tom, the mouse killer coming, they headed for higher grounds to the belfry. They had never heard the funeral dirge for *Whom the Bells Tolls*. Stalking the little squealers, he soon made short work of all the gnawing friends. Eating pie in the sky, old Tom drank a toast to all the stiffs, lying in state. If that wasn't a pop-eyed shindig as we buried the tiny streakers in our back yard. As for Tom, who was licking his chops with relish, I figured there was no one to cry over the poor little critters, but me.

Daddy, always a Jim-Dandy, all duded up, cut quite a figure, cutting a rusty in his prime all over the dance floor, or so I heard over the grapevine. With all the pretty young things hanging on his arms, do-si-do and swing that pretty girl around the floor and promenade all the way home, could be heard a country mile. Daddy was a lover, not a fighter, a swinger, and a macho man before Mama roped and bridled him. He always told us kids, Mama was his Little Sweetie Pie, cute as a button. In 1927, two years after my birth, Mama moved to the Big House in the sky.

Relying on Sis from then on, Daddy always knew what side his bread was buttered on, for he had to keep on the good side of Sis, his chief cook and bottle washer, his live-in babysitter.

As for our teenage brother, he was always kicking up his heels in some farmers back forty, seeking out his own little Sweetie Pie he could sink his teeth into. Peaches and cream with a dab of ice-cream on top, honey on the side, was his favorite dish. Honey he stole right out of the hive until he captured the "Queen Bee" that is—he got the sweetest of the sweet. Nuff said as the years rolled on.

In the 1930's, our house rested on stilts and looked like Long Tall Sally with her naked leg's exposed to the elements. The Mississippi River, within walking distance, often overflowed as it played a musical number beneath our sleeping quarters. *Water, water everywhere, and not a drop to drink.* The next day, paddling out in our little puddle jumper, we almost missed the boat. Reaching dry ground, however, was a sight for sore eyes. Dry sod at last, we camped out on our kinfolks back porch. The sun shining at our back a week later, breaking out the trusted guitar, never far from Daddy's side, we began to sing a spiritual, "It Ain't Gonna Rain No Mo'." Home never looked so good.

The old jalopy we drove had a leak in its get a-long that only hit on fours and sixes. Had very little juice-a-lene in its reservoir. The tires were often as flat as a pancake and already had half-a-dozen Band-Aids attached to its rubber inner tube. It had to have a big drink of water several times on any given trip; otherwise, it would get hotter than a firecracker, and blow its stack to kingdom come and back. Great balls of fire, how the steam rolled across the countryside. We waited and we waited for its gauge to fall. Cranking that old derelict, nobody knew when the motor would kick in. When it did, it would kick like a mule. Hot and bothered, mad as hornet, brother Herbert, who was the only one strong enough to crank it, would turn on that stubborn auto, give it a hefty kick right back, wearing hard toed brogan boots, right there in front of God and everybody. Missing its beat all the way, coughing and sputtering, I guess you could call it getting even steven.

Saturday was our weekly trip to the Big City, as we dubbed our small town. With moo-la jingling in our pockets, wearing our Sunday best, we were the cat's meow. Bouncing around in that old Model A Ford with a taste of flying dirt in our mouth, a stiff wind blowing through our hair, we were in hog heaven. Losing the cotton picking blues, Herbert, Sis, and I, sang a dirty little ditty called, *Dem Ole Cotton Fields Back Home*. With tattered and worn seat covers, a broken spring or two tickling our backside, dreaming big, we never saw anything ugly about Sally Goodun, for she was our chauffeur driven limo. Herbert, being the chauffeur was all spruced up fit to kill. Daddy was a home-body as he liked to putter around the farm. Cars were not his thing. He'd rather have a horse.

OOGA-OOGA was Sally Goodun's best feature as we blew into town. We were a big joke to the man on the street, as he shouted out, "Ah, blow your nose. It sounds better." We didn't take too kindly to that. Nevertheless, we made it to the grocery store and the five and dime, our destination, tooting right down the middle of Main Street.

All in all, I guess you could call us a well-rounded, All-American family. There was nothing square about us country bumpkins. Hollywood had nothing on us. Punch drunk on all the fun in town, we loaded up and hit the road for home. There I was with a half-eaten candy bar in my pocket, grape soda staining my mouth and a gob of bubblegum stuck in my hair, my dress looking like last week's dirty laundry. Lying half in and half out of Sister's big lap, drooling all over her pretty, rumpled dress, I was snug as a bug in a rug, sleeping like a baby. As darkness closed in around us, silence surrounded us except for the chug-a-lug of Sally Goodun's motor, and a frog choir blasting out their love song. Flying down that wind-swept road, dust boiling up behind us, causing a heat wave, who cared. Hitting a pot hole in the middle of the road, I woke up long enough to see Sis lean over me, give me a big smooch on my grubby cheek and hear her say, "Poor little angel! I guess Sister's been a little too hard on you, over-doing the Green Tea thing a bit." Giving me a loving smile, she cuddled me closer in her warm embrace. My last waking thought before I dropped off to sleep again was, by golly, Miss Molly. Sis was a pretty good old gal after all.

Herbert was lost in his own fantasy world of wine, women and song. We rolled into our little island retreat as Sally Goodun's light went out and so did mine.

My Sister/Mother

Our mother passed away at the age of thirty-three years in 1927. Leaving her husband, Herman, a son, Herbert, and two daughters, Walene and Euple to mourn her passing.

From that day forth, my twelve-year-old sister took over the role of motherhood for me, her two-year-old sibling. My big sister was all things to me. She was not only my beloved sister, she was the mother who rocked me to sleep. I felt secure with my hand in hers. She wiped my snotty nose, dried my tears. When I was sick, she sat by my bedside day and night, bathing my fevered brow. Tucked me into bed at bedtime with a kiss and a good night. Her favorite bedtime refrain was, "Sleep tight, don't let the bedbugs bite."

She was also the one who poked that vile tasting medicine down my throat for one ailment or another. Epsom Salts was her favorite remedy that I hated with dread and tears. It was like trying to corral a bucking horse to make me swallow that nasty concoction that smelled even worse.

She was also my guidance counselor, all that I am or hope to be, I owe to my Sister-Mother. Sorry to say I was often a pain in her neck. More so I suppose than I ever realized.

Sister was young enough to be my playmate, my best friend, my buddy. She was also my favorite teacher, my health nurse, my role model. Using her as an example, I tried to pass her values on to my five, beautiful children. I hope I have been an influence in the lives of my grandchildren.

She taught me Biblical principals that I've tried to live by. She tried to teach me how to be a Lady. Being the tom-boy that I was, I often rebelled at her lessons when she reminded me a Lady didn't climb trees, play rough and tough games, ride a stick horse, play cowboy and Indians, jump a rope, especially around boys, for my dress would fly up and show my underwear. That sure wasn't a Lady-like thing to do. Playing marbles with the boys, squatting around on the ground was frowned upon as well. Swinging from the rafters of the barn loft with the smell of stale dust in my hair with hay and cobwebs clinging to my clothes was a no-no. My dress really got a work-out at my monkey shines while playing in the barn. Being a Lady was no fun at all. Who

165

wanted to be a Lady anyway? I certainly didn't. Boy things were the epitome of fun.

There has never been a time in my life, Sis has not been there. She guided me through the terrible twos, my school days, my teenage years, my marriage, the birth of five children. She was there at the death of our Dad, my beloved husband, Joe, and our brother, Herbert, and other members of our family. I'm thankful I was there sharing her grief when her husband, Carmie, died. I felt I could pay a little back by being her support for a change. She has been there sharing our golden years together. Often with a loving pat on my shoulder, or else we cried together over some long forgotten memory or new tragic event. Yet we've laughed much more than we cried. I wonder how many tears she possibly shed for the family—tears we never saw.

When I think of her, I think of the phrase I've often heard: "Love is a many splendored thing." In my childhood when a little girl's favorite doll or coveted toy got broken or misplaced, when I got hurt as was often the case, I'd repeat the same old song day after day: "Sister, fix it." She almost always worked her magic, sending me away with a smile and a kiss. Even after I grew up, Sis was the one who could fix my problems. If she couldn't it was left up to my husband or my brother to fix. In eighty-one years, I have never lost faith in her ability and knowledge to put things right. She could make the sun shine once again. Truly, she had been my fixer upper and a beloved servant to her little family.

The birth of her own son in 1955 at the age of thirty-nine brought joy and Christmas all combined when she held that little boy in her embrace. Billy Wayne was everything she ever dreamed of and more. The economy was much better by then and she didn't have to juggle every penny that came in. She could afford to dress him up in a store-bought suit and tie and show him off to her family and friends. Man! If he didn't look sharp! He was her little man. Hollywood kids never looked so good. She guided and prodded him through countless music lessons where he learned to tickle the keys of the piano with finesse.

She lived for the hours she could hear sweet music waft through the house under his talented fingers. To her untrained musical ear, it was enough for her that she could share in his glory.

When her grandchildren came along, she treasured every golden moment she spent in their presence. Holding them close in her embrace was magic and a little bit of Heaven on Earth. They were what dreams and love were made of, especially when they said, "I love you, Granny."

I know the feeling, for I was often in her home, sharing my children along with her, our hearts beat as one in our happiness. Did she ever feel like a servant to all of us? No, I don't believe she ever did, for she was the queen of her domain, basking in the kingdom of her court. It was her privilege to be surrounded by our princely presence.

Never once in all those years did I ever hear her complain about her lot in life. Yes, she was one of a kind, salt of the earth. Her determination and brave spirit never faltered or failed, she was always right there in the buggy.

Even though Sis had no ear for music, or song, she gloried in her son's and her grandchildren's musical talent. How proud of her own performers she was as the glory did roll when her favorite song, "Beulah Land," rang out over the congregation at church, or an all day singing.

Yet I believe Sis had a beautiful song locked away in her soul. From childhood, she listened to the symphony of life that she so willingly shared with her family and many friends. June 24, 2007, I believe that song burst forth like a flood when she looked into the face of Jesus Christ and was in perfect rhythm with the angel's song.

I remember the hours she spent slaving over a wood burning cook stove, preparing our meals three times a day, summer and winter. Those meals were always on time, johnny on the spot as she dished out our food. Ah, the back breaking hours she spent bending over a tub and rub board full of dirty clothes on wash day. The next day, standing by that same hot stove, she ironed everything, and I mean everything, to the dish towels, wash cloths, sheets and pillow cases and even our underwear didn't escape.

Daddy and Herbert's snow white shirts were starched and pressed to the nth degree. Never let it be said our wardrobe and other things blowing in the breeze, had tattle-tale gray. Tattle-tale gray was a disgrace—big time!

I can still smell the aroma that came from that old wood burning monster that ate tons of wood when she made her famous biscuits and gravy, along with other goodies. Those biscuits slathered with sweet butter were a meal by themselves. Those mouth-watering gold nuggets made one go back for more. Her cakes and pies made from scratch would make McDonald's and Wendy's hang their head in shame. They were always picture perfect and tasted slap-alicious.

Cooking, cleaning (always a clean freak) and taking care of her motherly duties, and keeping Daddy and Herbert in line were at the top of the list. She went right along with the men to work in the fields for a mere pittance. She wielded a hoe in spring and a cotton sack in the fall, all the while, sweating her way down those old tall cotton rows, carrying a heavy load of the white stuff on her back.

How well I remember those old, much used wooden floors, had to sparkle until one could just about see their reflection. No one dared walk across them until they were completely dry and there better not have been mud on the feet. Muddy feet were strictly taboo and not allowed in her house.

The goose down feather bed we inherited from our mother was covered with snow white *ironed* sheets and clean covers. All of which was home made of course. When one sank down in that soft comfort, it was like sleeping on a cloud. Every day though, those beds were made up with another white top sheet to grace its contours. No one had better touch that work of art throughout the daylight hours. Unless, of course, one of us was sick, then we got the royal treatment of a bedside nurse. Otherwise, we had to lay on a well-used quilt in the floor we called a pallet.

On rainy days, Mama's sewing machine could be heard far into the night, turning out our wardrobe. The little girl I was at the time, I felt like I stepped out of the pages of a Sears and Roebuck catalog, as I wore one of her creations. I was Cinderella as a Princess, all decked out in my finery. Sis was determined her house and her family looked as well as any of our neighbors, even if it killed her. A self-made seamstress, she was the envy of all her peers.

She sent me off to school in the fall and winter warmly dressed, starched and pressed, smelling like Palmolive soap and with a well-filled lunch pail. It contained a simple meal, yet it was seasoned with love.

Her schooling was cut short in order that I could get the education she never got. From that first day in that little country school, I was fascinated with words and pictures on a big colorful chart. Learning to read became the love of my life. I later went on to read tales of *Robinson Crusoe*, *Robin Hood*, *Huckleberry Finn*, and *Treasure Island*. I'd take those books home and share them with Sis. Night after night, we devoured those printed words by a kerosene lamp. My favorite stories were about a princess who lived in a castle or knights in shining armor riding magnificent horses. Although a princess in a book had nothing on me. I had my own living princess in our little country castle. Besides, I never could conjure up images of a make-believe princess anyway.

My heart felt thanks and more to my princess who gave me the gift she never got. Ah, the sacrifice she made and the long hours she spent taking care of her family and house, while her teenage friends were out having fun with nothing more to do than flirt with the boys. If, and when, she did go out, she was never completely satisfied till she got back home with her charges—where we all belonged for heaven's sake.

Yet through the school of hard knocks, she earned her PhD in child philosophy. Home economics was a required subject where she excelled at the top of the class. It was a struggle to get her degree in agriculture. She often had to study from sun up to sun down, with a break for lunch. Learning the difference between commerce and dividend was a hard taskmaster—as she labored over the cost of living. On top of her other achievements, she had to take a course in deportment to learn how to be a loving respectable daughter and a good sister to Herbert and I. In that course, she graduated with flying colors.

I hope I have never brought shame or disrespect on those big shoulders of hers. Yet, she loved me and understood any wrong doing I did and forgave me. She loved me like I was her own daughter. Indeed, I felt like I was. I can truthfully say I was never deprived of love and forgiveness.

I cannot leave you here, Sis, for there has to be a sequel to the life you have lived.

When we all sit down at the King's table, it won't be complete without a huge pan of hot biscuits, setting smack-dab in the middle of that humongous table, along with a huge bowl of lick-em dab (gravy) and all sorts of healthy food to tickle our taste buds. I can see you now, hovering around nearby, waiting on the table. You are going to lean over my shoulder as you often did and whisper in my ear, "Eat, Euple. Sister fixed it."

Never again will I have to be alone as we often were as young children due to the fact Daddy and Herbert were working and living away from home. We have been alone many times after our mates passed away and the children left the nest. Surely you have earned your reward, Sis. Now that your blinded eyes are open, you are seeing the beauty of heaven and in perfect rhythm with the song of the angels, singing "Beulah Land," with abandonment and pleasure.

As for me, when I join you, I'll hear the trumpet from heaven distinctly without any trouble, for my hearing will be recovered once again. Then the Riney and Caldwell family will celebrate Heaven's Jubilee.

Sis, I've always loved you. Always and forevermore.

Dedicated to Walene Caldwell—July 12, 1916-June 24, 2007. May the angels be her servants now.

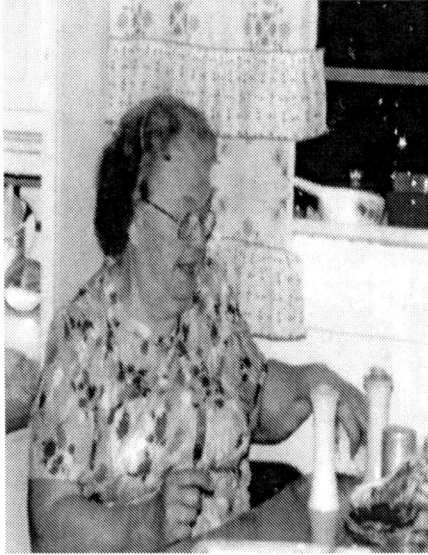

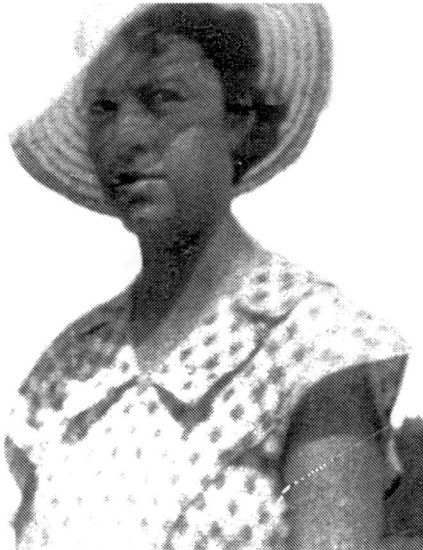

Walene Caldwell

TOOK fizick
mon.

Printed in the United States
91126LV00002B/97-195/A

9 780937 660362